The DAMAGE *of* DECEPTION

Brenda Rogers

First Edition

NEWMAN SPRINGS PUBLISHING
320 Broad Street
Red Bank, NJ 07701

First originally published by Newman Springs Publishing 2019

ISBN 978-1-64531-138-6 (Paperback)
ISBN 978-1-64531-139-3 (Digital)

Printed in the United States of America

Chapter 1

The loud talking coming from downstairs awoke me, quickly checking my alarm clock, let me know I forgot to set it... Wow! When did all these people arrive? Today was my mother's wedding day. This day had been planned for over a year now and just in a few hours, it would be over.

Looking at my maid of honor's dress that hung on my bedroom door, it was so pretty and big—which could be my downfall today if I choose to let it—but today, I choose not.

After a quick shower, I went downstairs. It looked like a family reunion; only thing was, I didn't know none of them. Everyone was talking to me at once. All I could manage to say was it's nice to meet you too. I didn't know these people. I mean, I knew they were my family, but to me, they were strangers.

I was not used to having a big family around; I wasn't used to having a small family around.

I knew my mother had a big family, but this was the first time I have ever met them.

Aunts, uncles, and cousins, they all seem to be one big happy family. But to me, they were invading my house and my life, but they were so nice.

As a child, I never questioned Mom about her family. But as I got older, I would often ask her about her brothers and sisters, her mom and dad, but she would only tell me they lived very far away, and they had their own lives.

I immediately liked them. I especially liked my aunt Judy because she looked so much like my mother. Her husband, my uncle

Rob, which was very talkative, he started telling me all kinds of things I did not know about my mother. Uncle Rob was a pastor of a big church in Iowa. The very same church my mother and all her siblings and my grandparents attended.

In fact, Uncle Rob told me that my grandfather was the pastor there until he passed away. I never knew my grandparents, nor did I know my mother went to church. And it's funny I only have one memory of going to church as a child. It was right after my dad had left us.

A lady that Mom worked with took us to her church.

I can also remember being in a Sunday school class. And for some reason, I never forgot the story the Sunday school teacher had told us. It was about a boy named Joseph and his father had made him a coat of many colors, and his brothers didn't like him.

I often wondered why we never went back because I really liked that church. And now today, I'm finding out that my mom was raised in church and that her father, my grandfather, was the pastor. Then my aunt Judy told me that my mother sang in a choir and how much she loved the church. But growing up, there was not even a Bible in our house.

Why hadn't my mother told me about this part of her life, the good part?

There was so much I didn't know, but I wanted the answers to my forever questions. Now I think I found just that person to answer them, Aunt Judy.

After getting a cup of coffee, I headed for the garage, which for today was a dressing room and a beauty parlor. Mother's family all lived out of state. So every motel and hotel around was filled with our family members.

I was only five years old when my dad walked out on us. Whenever I would ask about him, my mom would always tell me he was working out of town. Now I know she was telling me half of the truth; he was working out of town. She just never told me he also had another family out of town. I found that out later on in life. I remember one day, she told me daddy was not coming home anymore but that he loved me very much. As long as I could remember, he was never at home. So I never missed him. As a matter of fact, I liked it when he went away because when he was at home, he made my mom cry a lot, and he was always yelling at me. I was scared of him. So when he went away, I had peace.

It has been mother and I my whole life, and that was okay with me. She was my best friend. We had been through a lot together. There were times I would come home from school crying because of kids being so cruel to me. There was this one time, a girl—that called herself my friend—started calling me names. The rest joined in on the name-calling. She said no one wanted to be my friend because I was so fat, and they were afraid that my mother and I would eat them like we ate everything else. That hurt me so much.

I had always wondered if my dad left my mom because of her weight. He was always calling her names, and it seemed to be toward her being overweight. He used to tell her that I was going to be just like her if she didn't stop feeding me so much. But to me, my mom was beautiful.

I missed a lot of school growing up because I hated it so much and would come up with so many reasons why I couldn't go, and it was mostly because of other kids. The name-calling and not having any friends was really hard on me.

I think there was some kind of rule in school about not having a fat kid for a friend. A rule no one ever broke. Like my mother, I have been overweight my whole life, and it didn't help coming home to an empty house every day. After school, I would come home, watch TV, and eat. My mother would always go to bed early because she would have to get up early.

But I think she went to bed early because she was so unhappy. I would hear her crying after she closed her bedroom door. So I would stay up, watch TV, and eat.

Chapter 2

Then like overnight, everything seemed to change. Mom started working nights at the factory. At first, she didn't want to change shifts. But after a while, she didn't seem to mind it.

I would be in bed when she would come home, but I could hear humming, and then I could hear her making coffee. She would always be on the phone, talking to someone. I could never hear what she was saying, but I could hear her laughing a lot.

On the weekends, we would take long walks together. She started buying healthy foods. she seemed so happy, and that made me happy.

I looked forward to our walks; we would walk and laugh. She told me that after we lost some weight, we could go shopping for new clothes. We went to the movies. It was like a whole new life.

I never asked her, but I wondered who she was talking to every night until late. Who was it on the other end of the phone that had made her change so much? Well, it didn't take long to find out.

One Saturday, she told me someone was going on our walk with us—someone she had met at work. His name was Bill, and he wanted to meet me. So that day, we waited on the front step for him. I had so many mixed emotions that day. I was glad that this man was making her happy, and I felt like I had my mom back. But I was losing her again. I never had to share her with anyone, and I was kind of scared.

When Bill arrived, mom's whole face lit up.

"Well, hello, you must be Tina. You are as beautiful as your mother," Bill sayid

Okay...one point for him!

Bill talked, and the two of them laughed during our whole walk. It was like being with teenagers. I had never seen my mom giggle so much.

After our walk, I told Bill that it was nice to meet him, and I went inside. They sat on the porch for a long time, then he left. I really didn't know what to say when Mom asked me what I thought of Bill. I mean, he was nice and all; I just didn't want her to get hurt again. It took years for her to stop crying after Dad left, and it had only been just recently that she put away Dad's pictures. But who was I to say anything? So I told her I liked him; that seemed to make her happy.

"Bill wants to take us out for supper tonight," Mom said, all excited.

"Oh, Mom, why don't you just go? I will fix me something here. There is a movie I want to see tonight." A lie.

"Come on, Tina, please come with us," she pleaded, "I want you to get to know Bill. He is a great guy."

"All right, I will go," I told her, even though I did not want to.

I wasn't used to eating at restaurants, especially nice ones. Bill kept me in their conversations; he asked me all kinds of questions about myself. He really seemed to have a sincere interest in how I felt about things. I think we talked more than mother did. I must say I had a great time, and I was glad I came. So after that night, Bill was over a lot, and I didn't mind. I liked Bill. He became a big part of my life.

The three of us still took long walks together; he cooked us nonfat meals that was actually good.

Bill lived in a big house in the country, and that was where we spent most of our weekends.

There were long trails that went through the woods; it was great. We were losing weight, and for the first time in my life, I had a family.

It was like Bill had rescued us, and I was so grateful to him; he was a kind man.

He never made me feel like I was just in the way. He was always including me in everything they did.

But after a while, I come to realize they didn't need me with them all the time. So when they would ask me to go somewhere with them or to watch a movie with them, I would make excuses not to. I knew my mother was in good hands, and I needed to give them time alone. But I must admit, I did miss spending time with them.

I did keep taking the weekend walks with them, and I did keep losing the weight.

It was so great when Mom and I went shopping for new clothes. It is true about the saying: when you look good, you feel good. I mean, I wasn't skinny by no means, but I had lost sixty-three pounds and I felt great. Mother had lost over ninety pounds, and she was beautiful. But of course, she has always been beautiful to me. But now, she was happy.

Chapter 3

On my eighteenth birthday, Bill and Mother took me out to a fancy restaurant, and it was so sweet when Bill came to pick us up. He gave me eighteen red roses.

A few weeks after my birthday, Bill and Mom announced they were getting married. I was very happy for them and for me. So after that, everything was about the wedding.

Mom didn't have a wedding with my dad; they ran away and got married by the justice of the peace. Bill told her she could have as big as a wedding as she wanted…so she went all out.

She talked to her sisters on the phone every day. She was so happy; she was like a different person. It's funny how love can change everything about a person.

One day, Mom told me that after my graduation, she was going to give me our house. I already had a job lined up at Mom's factory. I would be working in the office. I was so thrilled to have my very own house, now I just needed a car.

A few months before my graduation, Mom moved into Bill's house. We were there all the time anyway. I knew it was going to be hard for me because I didn't have a car, but again Bill helped me out. He told me to start looking for a car, and he would loan me the money for it. I wasn't crazy about the idea of borrowing money from him, but I didn't really have a choice.

We spent the weekend packing and getting Mom moved into Bill's house. She made sure I had plenty of food and everything else I needed before she left. And then she was gone.

I was happy for mom. I was happy for Bill, but it didn't ease the pain I felt when I laid down at night. I wanted what they had… I wanted love. I wanted someone to look at me the way Bill looked at my mother. I wanted a family of my own, a husband, and kids.

As I walked into the garage, my aunt was just finishing my mom's hair; she looked gorgeous. Her wedding dress was also gorgeous; the prettiest one I had seen and believe me in the last year, I have seen plenty.

"You're next," my aunt informed me. My best feature was my long hair. I was always getting compliments on my hair.

I grabbed a donut off the table on my way to my seat. It had been so long since I had tasted something so good. As I listened to my mom and aunts talk, I could tell there was a time when they were very close before my dad came along and took her away. I could also tell by the way they talked about my dad, they did not care for him at all. There was so much I didn't understand, like during my growing up years, why had I not ever met my mom's family? And why when they all lived hundreds of miles away, did we live here alone with no family, just my mother and I? And what kept her here after my dad left?

My life could have been so different maybe if I could have been around aunts, uncles, and cousins—around family. I just didn't understand, and I wanted answers. And if Mom didn't want to talk to me about it, then maybe Aunt Judy would.

The wedding went perfect. Bill had tears in his eyes when Mom walked down the aisle. The reception was held at a big hotel banquet hall. Everything was fancy and beautiful. They had a live band, but besides dancing with my uncles a few times, I just sat there, and people watched. Everyone was having a good time, and I had never seen my mom happier than she was today. I was glad when the time came for Bill and mom to leave for the airport; they were going to Florida for a week. Mom had always wanted to go there.

I had a bad headache and was so ready to go home. After telling all my aunts, uncles, and cousins goodbye because they were all leaving the next morning, I drove mom's car home. I felt bad that Aunt Judy was leaving before I got the chance to talk to her, but she gave me her phone number.

Chapter 4

The next morning, I slept later then I planned. After my shower, I started cleaning and rearranging the furniture. I still couldn't believe this was my house even though I grew up in this house. But now, it was all mine.

I had purchased some paint earlier this week. So after the cleaning was done, I painted the living room. Tomorrow I would do the kitchen and my bedroom. It looked so good.

It was getting late in the afternoon, and I realized I hadn't eaten, so I treated myself and went down to a little diner not far from home. I didn't want to go far because it would be dark when I came home.

After giving my order to the waitress, I sat there relaxing. I wondered what Mother and Bill was doing right now. I hadn't had time to miss her until now, and I felt the tears start to blur my vision.

Thankful that the waitress brought my food right then. That's when I noticed how pretty she was, even though she was overweight. She seemed so happy. Maybe being overweight wasn't my problem; it didn't seem to be hers.

The whole week went by very slow. I found that I didn't have a lot to do after I got home from school. I missed our walks, but I didn't want to walk alone. At the same time, I didn't want to gain any of my weight back that I had lost. I was real careful about what I ate, and I did walk around the house. I put my graduation gown on again and stood in front of the mirror. I didn't look too bad. I must admit. I was proud of myself.

I couldn't wait until after graduation to start my new job and to meet people—maybe even a guy. When Mom and Bill returned from their honeymoon, they looked more in love than before they left if that was possible. Bill and Mother gave me a little graduation party; a few of Mom's friends and Bill's friends came, even a few of my teachers stopped by, and that was all. But I was just happy Bill and Mom went to the trouble for me. I had the two people there that meant the world to me, and that was all that mattered.

After looking a few weeks in the newspaper trying to find a good used car. I think I may have found the right one. Anyway it sounded good, and it was in my price range. I called about it. A lady answered; she told me a little about it. She said it belonged to her daughter, and she had the car with her at her work right now, but I could go there and look at it. She also said she had a lot of calls on it.

So I called Bill right away, I didn't want to take a chance of someone buying it before I could. Bill said he would be here to pick me up as soon as he could.

The place the lady told me about was the little diner down from my house. From the description she gave me, I spotted the car right away. Little did I know that day that I wasn't just getting a car, I was about to meet someone who would change my life and become my best and only friend. It was the waitress that had waited on me that night. Her mom called her and told her we were coming down to look at the car, so she was waiting outside for us. She reached out her hand and introduced herself as Joan.

"Hi, I'm Tina, and this is my stepdad Bill." The words sounded strange as I said them. This was the first time I had called Bill dad.

As she unlocked the doors to the car, she told us about it and how she couldn't afford it on her pay and had no choice but to sell it. I felt sorry for her. That was the beginning of our friendship because later that day, after we signed the papers, I drove the car home. I found some things she had not gotten out of the car, so I went back to the diner to return them. She was just getting off of work and about to call her mom to pick her up, so I offered to give her a ride home.

We were a lot alike we discovered. On that ride to her house, she was an only child. She never knew her dad. It was just her and her mom; they had no other family here. She had a hard time in school like me; she never made friends easily. She had never dated, so we had a lot in common. I enjoyed being around Joan. She was very funny. I liked her.

The next day was her day off. We made plans to go to the mall and hang out. Wow, I had never hung out with anyone but my mother.

Chapter 5

My first day at my job went pretty good. The people were very friendly. There was so much to learn. I did some bookkeeping in the office at school, but this was a whole different ball game. I knew it wouldn't take me long to get the hang of it. I hoped anyway.

I didn't see Mom much at work, just in passing. As I was coming to work, she was leaving. I felt my life was changing for the better; I had my own place, a car, a job, and now a friend—someone I could hang out with and talk to. I was happy, and my mother was happy.

Joan and I hung out just about every weekend when she didn't have to work. I would pick her up. We would go to eat, go to the mall. It was fun, and then some nights, we would go to the video store, rent a movie or two, grab some fast food, and go back to my house. We would stay up most of the night and sleep late the next day.

I was gaining my weight back. I didn't walk anymore, and I was eating way too much fast food. I knew things had to change.

One Sunday afternoon, I was on my way to Mom's for dinner. I saw my chance to change things. A new club was opening in our town, featuring a live band. It sounded great and a lot of fun. I couldn't wait to tell Joan about it. I just hoped she was ready for a change also. I had a nice dinner and visit with my parents. I missed coming here. I even missed his dogs and the country.

On my way home, I stopped to read the sign at a closer view; it says it will be open at the end of the month, which was three weeks from now.

I called Joan as soon as I got home and told her all about it. She didn't sound too excited about it at all, but she said she would give it a try. I couldn't wait, and I knew soon she would be just as excited as I was. Neither one of us knew how to dance, but it was going to be fun learning.

The next day, after work, I picked Joan up, and we went to the video store. We looked around for a DVD to teach us how to dance, but the only DVD teaching dance was a DVD on line dancing. The lady there said it was the latest thing; everyone was line dancing nowadays, so we rented it.

We got something to eat, went back to my place to watch the tape. It looked like fun, but I had my doubts we could ever learn to dance like that. It didn't look easy, but we were going to try. I had rented the DVD for a week, so after we ate, our first practice began.

After two hours of practice, we were having a blast. It was easier than we thought, and a well workout that I needed. We practiced every night for two whole weeks, then we went shopping for new outfits. We were going to be ready when the club opened. Now all we needed was the courage to go.

The closest I had ever been to a dance floor or club was at Mom and Bill's wedding. Then Joan said something to me I hadn't even thought about my age. Joan was old enough, but what if I couldn't even get into the club. That would suck.

The night of the club opening, the parking lot was packed. We were so scared and excited. We made our way up to the door. The man asked for our identification. After showing him, he put a wristband on me and stamped my hand, so they wouldn't serve me. That was okay because I wasn't planning on drinking anyway; I just came to dance.

The music was loud, and the dance floor was full. We found a little table and sat down. The waitress came over and took our orders.

"Two cokes please."

I told Joan there is no way I'm getting on that dance floor. And I knew I had made a big mistake coming here, but Joan's eyes were all lit up like a kid on Christmas morning. What have I done?

Joan had a good time no matter where she was. I just wanted to go home. Before I could tell her that, she was on the dance floor.

"Come on, Tina!" she yelled over the noise.

I just kept shaking my head no. I knew the dance they were doing, but I could not make myself get up there. After a while, Joan stop asking me. Well, I'm glad one of us was having fun.

That night, the only time I saw Joan was when she came to the table for her drink or when the band took a break.

"Tina, you don't know what you are missing. You know the dances, and this was your idea, remember?" Tina said.

"Yes, I remember, but I just can't. I'm sorry, Joan, I don't want to disappoint you, but I just can't get up there."

On the way home, Joan talked about nothing else. She was so excited about coming back next weekend, and again I asked myself, *What have I done?*

Chapter 6

The next weekend was about the same; all though there wasn't as many people as last weekend. The dance floor was still pretty full. I did feel more comfortable. I still couldn't bring myself to get on the dance floor. Like before, I sat and watched everyone else having fun. I wanted so much to dance with Joan and the others, but I just didn't have the guts. Joan didn't seem to notice anymore that I just sat there. Once, I even saw her slow dancing with a guy.

After work on Monday, I went by myself and got a new outfit. I had my nails done; my hair trimmed and highlighted. All week I did the line dancing DVD. Even if I never got the nerve to get on the dance floor, I was going to look good and get my workouts doing the video if nothing else.

On Friday night, when Joan called me to see if I wanted to go to the club, even though I had already changed my mind not to go, I told her yes. She said her mom was going to drop her off at my house. I was just about to step into the tub when I heard her knock at the door. Putting a towel on, I opened the door for her. She was carrying a bag.

"Guess what I have," she said, taking out orange juice and a bottle of something.

"What is this? Are you drinking?" I asked.

"I've only had one drink. Come on, Tina, it will help you relax."

"Have you ever had a drink before?" I asked.

"Just a few times, no big deal," she said.

So I let her fix me a drink, and I carried it to the bathroom with me. As I took my bath, I took a sip. It kind of burned on the way down, but it tasted good and before I knew it, she brought me another one. It made me feel pretty good. I liked it, and I liked the way it made me feel.

On the way there, Joan drove, and I could not stop laughing. Joan kept telling me to get it together, or they weren't going to let me in the club. We got a table across from the bar. It didn't seem to be so loud as before. The dance floor was already packed. One sip from Joan's drink, and she was gone. I wish I had her guts; maybe in time, I would. But for now, I was feeling good just being here.

That was the night Paul Sanford walked into the club and changed my every thought, my very way of thinking. It was love at first sight. A lot of people seem to know him. Everyone was going up to him and talking to him. Try as I might, I couldn't stop looking at him. I mean he was sitting right across from me. I wanted to change tables and sit somewhere else, but I couldn't move. I was so aware he was there. He never looked my way. I just wanted to go home. But instead, I spend the rest of the night trying not to look at him. He didn't dance, even though I did see girls go up and talk to him. I just assumed they were asking him to dance. I was kinda sad when he got up and walked out the door. I wondered if I would ever see him again.

Later on, after the club started getting empty, Angie, a waitress there, came by my table to clean it off. And before I thought, I asked her about the guy sitting at the bar earlier.

"Oh, you mean Paul?" she said.

"Yes, I think that's his name." I didn't want her to know I already knew his name.

"That's Paul Sanford. He used to come here a lot before this place closed down. I mean before the new owners took over and reopened it. What would you like to know?"

"I don't know," I said, "I was just wondering if you knew anything about him."

"Well, I know he went through a bad divorce. He is a construction worker. He works out of town a lot. He is a real sweet guy, never gives me any trouble. That's about all I know, sweetie."

"Thank you," I said.

Joan came back to the table. "Come on, Tina, dance with me. No one is going to be looking at you. It's fun. Come on!" she pleaded.

I wanted to so very bad. I knew the dances they were doing like the back of my hand. I did them every night at home. So I got up and followed Joan to the dance floor. And I had so much fun. At first, I made a few mistakes, but I didn't care, and no one seem to notice. It seem like the song was over so fast; I didn't want to stop. I had just gotten started. We danced every fast songs and before I knew it, it was time to leave.

I couldn't believe these last few weeks, I missed out on this. It was so fun, now I couldn't wait until tomorrow night. Usually we only came one night on the weekend, but that was before I knew how much fun this was and before I laid eyes on Paul.

Joan spent the night with me. The next day, we went over our dance steps. I took a long time getting dressed and had a few drinks. I wanted to be ready just in case maybe, just maybe, Paul was there; I wanted to look my best.

As we pulled in to the parking lot of the club, I saw Paul getting out of his truck. My heart took a flip. How could I have these feelings over someone I had only seen once?

We got our table. Joan ordered a drink, and I ordered a coke. I wish I was old enough to get a drink; I sure needed one tonight.

All the time I was on the dance floor, I kept my eye on Paul. I hope he wouldn't leave early like he did last night. He didn't dance; he just sat there and watched everyone. But before the band was over, he left.

On the way home, Joan asked me, "What was up with the guy at the bar?"

"What do you mean?" I said.

"Oh, come on, Tina, you couldn't take your eyes off of him all night."

"I just thought he was cute, but I didn't keep my eyes on him all night!"

"Yeah, you did. So why don't you ask him to dance?"

"Oh, right…like I'm going to go up to a stranger and say… Would you like to dance? Sure, Joan!"

"And what's wrong with that?" she said.

"Let's see, when he says no thanks…and I have to crawl under the table until he leaves. No, thanks! Besides he has never noticed me, and why should he."

"You need to stop putting yourself down, Tina. You are a very pretty girl."

"Thanks, Joan."

Chapter 7

All week at work and at home, Paul was on my mind. I would catch myself dreaming about him. The following Friday night was about the same; I danced a lot and watched Paul sat at the bar, went home feeling kind of down.

Next Saturday was my birthday. I had a feeling Joan was giving me a party at the club because the other day, Mom—not meaning to, of course—said, "I'll give you your gift at the club this Saturday."

I was looking forward to it because if I was having a party, then Paul would have to notice me if he is there.

On Saturday, Joan came over around four o'clock, bringing me a few birthday drinks. she gave me a very pretty sweater for my birthday. "I thought you might want to wear this tonight."

"Thank you very much. It's beautiful," I said.

"So are you ready for your big night?"

"I am," I said, "I'm very excited."

"Good because this is not my only gifts to you."

"What do you mean?"

"Oh, you will see later."

That was all she would tell me. But all the time we were getting ready, Joan was smiling. I'm glad she didn't know that I had already guessed about the party she was giving me.

When we walked into the club that night, I acted shocked. There were balloons, decorations, a cake, gifts, and lots of people sitting at the birthday table.

Paul would have to notice me tonight. I watched the door, and Paul didn't show up. Of all nights, he chose this one not to come.

I tried not to show my disappointment, and I did have great time anyway. It was the first time Mom and Bill had been here. It was nice to see them dance and enjoy themselves. I had almost forgot about Paul—almost.

At the end of the night, everyone had left but Joan and I. I was very tried and was ready to call it a night. I knew I was never going to meet the man that kept me awake nights. I also knew it would have to be me that made the first move or get him out of my head, and the only way I could do that was to stop coming here. But I didn't want my old life back. Oh well, I would think of some way to stop thinking of him somehow because I knew I would never get the courage to ever approach Paul.

As Joan and I were walking out the door that night, Paul was walking in. "Happy birthday, Tina," he said.

"Thank you," I mumbled and kept walking. I didn't know what else to do. I thought for sure Joan was going to have to carry me to the car because my legs were like rubber bands.

Joan started laughing. "Why didn't you talk to him? Instead of acting like you just came face-to-face with a ghost, this was your chance."

"I know, I know, but I couldn't. He took me by surprise. How did he even know my name? I was so shocked. All I could say was thank you."

"And you did that pretty well. I mean I was right beside you, and I barely heard you," Joan joked.

"Well, now he probably thinks I'm just stuck-up or crazy."

Chapter 8

The whole week, I couldn't eat, I couldn't sleep, I kept hearing over and over Paul's voice. "Happy birthday, Tina." Oh yes, it was a happy birthday.

I lived for Friday night. I didn't think it would ever get here, but it did. I already had what I was wearing laid out. I had stopped after work and had my nails touched up. I made myself a drink and got into a warm bubble bath. I went over in my mind my approach for tonight. I knew if he turned me down, I would just die of humiliation.

After a few more drinks, I think I had just the confidence I needed to approach him.

Joan picked me up in her mom's car because I asked her to. I wasn't taking any chances because if Paul did what I was hoping he would do, he would be driving me home tonight. When we pulled up at the club, right away I started looking for his truck, and there it was… My heart skipped a beat; he was here. I knew tonight had to be now or never, and of course, fear over took me when we walked in, and I saw him sitting there.

We sat down at a table, and Angie took our order. Even though I kept telling myself I was going to do this, I didn't trust myself to carry out my plans. So I sat there and waited for the band to play a slow song and when they did play a slow one, I waited for the next one.

I looked over at where Paul had been sitting, and he was looking this way; it even looked like he was looking at me, but I couldn't be sure. Then he got up and started walking toward me; my heart fell to the floor. I knew I had to pull myself together.

"Would you like to dance?" he said.

I don't remember answering him. I just remember being in his arms and feeling his breath so very close to my face and the smell of his aftershave. Then the song was over, and he walked me back to my table and said, "Thanks, Tina."

I felt like an idiot. I didn't say one word to him. Did I just blow the one chance I had been waiting for with Paul? What was wrong with me?

A few minutes later, Angie came over and placed a coke in front of me, and she said, "This is from Paul."

I looked at him, and he was smiling at me. He came over again and asked me to dance. But this time, I did talk or rather answered questions about myself. He told me he was divorced, he was a construction worker, he didn't like to fast dance, and he has lived in this town his whole life.

The song ended, and again he said, "Thank you." He walked me back to my table.

On the way home that night, I couldn't stop talking. I was on cloud nine. This was definitely a night I was not soon to forget.

Chapter 9

The next evening, Paul called me. I was so shocked to see his name on my caller ID. I know my voice was shaking when I said hello. He told me Joan had given him my phone number. He said he hoped it was okay that he called me. Wow! if he only knew…

We talked long into the night. He told me about his divorce. I could still hear the hurt in his voice. They had only been married a short time. He wanted kids, and she didn't. She had a son from a previous marriage, but his dad had custody, and she was trying to get him back. Paul felt like that was the reason she married him in the first place was just to get her son back, but he loved her. They had only dated a year before they married. Paul told me, as soon as she found out she wasn't getting her son back, things started going downhill for them. She started staying out all night. Then one day, he came home after being on a job out of town, and she had moved out, only leaving behind a note saying she had met someone else. He had never heard from her again. That was two years ago.

Paul told me a lot about himself that night, and I held on to every word. He told me both of his parents has passed away. He had an older sister; she lived in Florida with her husband and two kids. They had never been really close and only talked on holidays.

He told me when he has kids, he wanted two and close in age because it was so hard growing up with a sister so much older than him. He felt like he was an only child.

Everything he told me sounded like something I had been dreaming about my whole, like after we hung up, I laid awake for hours, replaying his every word. I don't know what time when sleep finally over took me, but I knew it was a sweet sleep. I knew no one would ever understand this, but I was already in love with Paul. He was all I could think about awake and asleep.

The next day at work was very hard. I was so tired I kept making mistakes. I couldn't focus on anything; I couldn't wait to go home and take a nap. When I finally did get home, there was a message on my answering machine from Paul. "Hey, Tina, hoping you are having a good day. I have been thinking about you. Well, the truth is… I haven't been able to get you off my mind."

I thought my heart was going to explode. I called him back. We made plans to go for supper the next night. I took a long hot bath and almost fell asleep in the tub, so this was what being in love felt like; my heart was so light, and sometimes I just laughed for no reason. I had never been this happy in my life.

After I went to bed, sleep went away and in its place came beautiful thoughts of Paul. I think I could recall every word he spoke to me because I have replayed them so many times in my mind.

The next evening, Paul picked me up, and he was such a gentleman, just as I knew he would be. He opened my car door for me, he pulled out my chair, and he looked so very nice—different for some reason, then at the club, better.

When we got back to my house, I invited him in for coffee, but he said he had to get up very early in the morning. I was so sure he was going to kiss me when he walked me to my door, but he just thanked me for having supper with him and said good night. Maybe he didn't feel the same way about me as I did about him. I knew it was crazy to even think about all this right now. We had just met, but I couldn't help it. I knew this had to be love.

Chapter 10

I was just about to get into the tub when Joan called me.

"Hey, just wanted to know if you want to go to the club Friday night?" she said.

"Sure, why not," I said. All I wanted was to be with Paul, but I didn't tell her that, and I was sure he would be at the club.

Another sleepless night thinking about Paul. I knew this had to stop. I could almost feel myself getting sick maybe because I couldn't eat or sleep. Besides, how is it possible to love someone you had just met? Maybe because this was the first guy that had ever looked my way or paid any kind of attention to me. I have noticed lately other guys looking at me, but it didn't matter now. I just wanted Paul looking my way. I also knew I didn't look like the girl I used to be; not only was I a lot lighter, I also had a new outlook on life, and I was happy—very happy.

The next day, Mom stopped by the office. I felt bad because I have so busy, I hadn't had a chance to go see her in a while.

"Hey, long time no see," she said.

"I know. I was just thinking about that," I said.

"So what about this guy you have been seeing?"

I could kill Joan for telling my mother about Paul. "Just one date with a friend. I don't know what Joan told you, but you know how she gets carried away about things," I said.

"So when are you going to bring him over to meet us?"

"Mother, it's not like we are dating. We went out to dinner one time. What will he think when I ask him to meet my parents?"

"Please, let him meet me first, or he's going to think I'm crazy."

The truth was, he would think I was crazy if he knew all the thoughts I had of him. Yes, even marriage thoughts, but I didn't say that out loud.

Friday night, when we pulled up at the club, I could have rejoiced when I saw Paul's truck. We walked in. Paul came walking toward us with a big smile on his face. He seemed happy to see me.

"Hi, Tina, I was going to call you today to ask you if you wanted to come here tonight, but I knew you always came with your friend, but I'm very happy to see you," he said.

I just stood there smiling at him.

"Are we going to be seated somewhere or stand here at the door all night?" Joan said with a smile.

So we followed her to a table. I wish I hadn't drove tonight, maybe Paul would ask to take me home. When we danced, Paul held me tight and a few times, I was sure he was going to kiss me. Oh, how I longed for that kiss.

Joan had met a guy; she had been dancing with him all night. There was just something about him I did not like; he was so flashy. And he couldn't seem to keep his hands off her.

Paul said he had to leave early, said he had to go out of town tomorrow to check on a job. That made me sad. Then he said he would be gone until Thursday; that made me sadder. Around ten o'clock, he said he had better go and asked me to walk with him to his car. Outside, he asked if he could call me.

"Yes, I would love for you to call me," I said. I told him I would miss him.

"I will miss you too. See you Thursday," he said, and he was gone. No kiss, no handshake, no hug, and no nothing.

I went back inside the club. I just wanted to go home. There was no point being here now with Paul being gone, but I had to stay and wait for Joan. By this time, she was all over that guy, so I asked her if maybe he could take her home.

"No, Tina, I can't let Mom know I'm with him. You know how she is. Please stay for just another hour, then we will go. I promise."

It was a very long hour. A guy asked me to dance, but I said no. I already missed Paul. I was worried about Joan and this guy. I didn't want her to get hurt. At the table, when Joan went into the restroom, he kept looking at me and smiling. He gave me the creeps.

"So what's going on with you and that guy? Is he your boyfriend?" he said.

"He is my friend," I said, looking toward the restroom, wishing Joan would hurry back.

"So you have no boyfriend. Is that what you are saying?" he said and then winked at me.

"No, that is not what I'm telling you, and I would appreciate it if you would stop looking at me." I was so happy to see Joan come back to the table. "Joan, I'm leaving now."

"Let her go, Joan. You can go home with me," he said as he stood up to leave.

"Okay, Tina, go on home. Tim will bring me to your house in the morning if that's all right with you," Joan said.

"Can I speak with you a minute, Joan?" I said. We walked away from Tim. "Look, Joan, you know this guy is no good for you. Please, let's just go. He is trouble."

"Tina, I really like him. I will be fine, just go and don't worry about me."

So I went home without her.

At three in the morning, Joan woke me, knocking on my door. I knew she had been crying, but she let me know right away she didn't want to talk about it. She went to bed.

The next morning, she acted like nothing was wrong. I took her home, and Tim's name was never once mentioned. When we got to her house, before she got out of the car, she said, "Tina, will you please go to the club with me tonight? Tim is going to meet me there."

"No, Joan! I do not want to go to the club again tonight. I don't want you to get hurt by Tim. He is a woman chaser. I'm only saying this because you are my friend, and I care about you."

Joan just gave me a mad look and said, "Well, thanks anyway."

"I will call you later," I said, but she just turned and walked away without another word.

On the way home, I thought about the situation, and I knew it wasn't my place to ask Joan not to see Tim. She is a grown woman, and I am not her mother. Plus I knew it was none of my business who she sees. At home, I called her and told her just that.

"I know you care about me, and I appreciate it. I really do. But Tim is not like that and if you would just give him a chance, I know you would like him," she said.

"Okay," I told her, "I will give him a chance, and if you want, I will drop you off at the club tonight, but I'm going to stay home tonight and catch up on some much-needed sleep."

"Thanks anyway, but Mom said I could use her car tonight."

"Okay, well, have fun."

Chapter 11

After all my housework and laundry was done, I made some popcorn and put a movie in. Ten minutes into the movie, the phone rang. It was Paul.

"Hey, I was thinking that you went out tonight," he said.

"Oh no, I decided to stay home tonight."

"I'm glad you did. Now we can talk," he said.

And that's what we did for hours a couple of times. I almost fell asleep, so around midnight, he said he had better go, or he would never get up in the morning. So after saying good night, I sat there thinking about all we talked about which was nothing new. We talked about our childhood, the movies and foods we liked. I did get the nerve to tell him my mother invited him to dinner, and to my surprise, he said he would love to go meet my parents. I think I went to sleep as soon as my head hit the pillow because. Now only three days until Thursday, and Paul.

The week seemed to drag by. I didn't hear from Joan, so I just assumed she was spending her time with Tim. Paul didn't call me back. I waited every night by the phone, just hoping.

On Thursday, while I was at work, Paul sent me flowers. It was so sweet of him; I almost cried when I read the note: "I miss you. Will you please have supper with me tonight?"

I called him on my lunch break to thank him for the flowers, and to say yes, I would love to have supper with him. After work, I rushed home to change. Paul took me to a very fancy restaurant, then to a movie. I wanted to reach out and hold his hand, but I was scared. What if he didn't want to hold my hand? He was so hard to read. I wondered why he never tried to kiss me or touch me. Maybe to him, I was only his friend. I had never been on a date with a guy, but this is sure not like it is in the movies.

After the movie, Paul took me home. He walked me to my door. "Would you like to come in for coffee or a coke?" I said.

"No, thank you, maybe another time. I need to get home and get to bed. It's been a long day. When do you want to go to your parents for dinner?"

"Whatever day is good for you," I said.

"Okay, how about Monday? If it's okay with your mom, of course."

"Oh, I'm sure that will be fine. I will call her tomorrow, and then I will let you know."

"Sounds good. Good night, Tina, it was good to see you again."

"Good night, Paul."

As I lay in bed, his words kept going through my mind. "It was good to see you again." What did he mean by that? It seemed the more I was with Paul; the more confused I was. Did he like me other than just a friend? Was I wasting my time with him? When he was away, I got the impression he felt the same way about me as I did about him, but when he was around me, I get the impression he only liked me as a friend.

I fell into a sleep dreaming about Paul. I didn't know when the night dreams became daydreams; all I knew was that he was on my mind at all times. I called mom about Monday. She said that would be fine. She was looking forward to meeting Paul. When I called Paul to let him know Monday evening was good, we only talked a few minutes because he was busy at work.

Chapter 12

After I got off work, I didn't go home. I went to Mom's. It had been awhile since I had been there, so I thought I would surprise them. Mom wasn't looking real good; she had dark circles under her eyes, and she just looked worn down. But when I said something about it, she told me she wasn't getting enough sleep. She said she had been working a lot over time, but she promised Bill she would slow down.

"Well, good," I said, "you don't need to make yourself sick by working too much."

"I know. Bill is always getting on my case about my work and my health. I can't wait to meet your friend, Paul."

We spent the next few hours talking about work, Paul, and my future—the perfect combination (work, Paul, and future). I so wanted Paul in my future.

"Tina, speaking of my health, what about you? How much weight have you lost? Don't you think it's time to stop dieting?"

"Well, I haven't been dieting. I just kinda of lost my appetite."

Then I remember Paul telling me in one of our phone conversations that he didn't like skinny women, but it was so hard for me to eat a lot these days, just a little food filled me up. I wasn't trying to lose more weight.

When I got home, there was two messages on my machine, one from Joan and one from Paul.

"Hey, where are you? I wanted to know if you want to go to the club tomorrow night, and no, I'm not meeting Tim. Tina, you were right. He is a loser. Call me. Bye."

I was glad she wasn't seeing Tim anymore.

"Hi, Tina, it's Paul. Call me when you get time."

Well, I have time now, so I dialed his number with a big smile. We talked and laughed for more than two hours. He told me he was looking forward to meeting my folks. He also invited me to go with him tomorrow; he had a job to check out. He told me there were lots of antiques shops we could stop at and check out. I told him I would love to.

"Great. Pick you up at 10:00 a.m.," he said.

"Okay, Paul, good night."

It was too late to call Joan. I would call in the morning before I left; she would understand. Well, I already knew there would be no sleeping for me tonight. I tried on everything in my closet, and when I finally did get to bed, I lay there thinking about Paul.

Paul and I had a good time. After his meeting—which didn't take long—we went to eat, and we took a walk in a park. I hoped Paul would hold my hand, but he made no move to do so. We went to a lot of antique shops; it was fun, not my usual Saturday.

The day went by much too fast. On the way home, we talked and laughed about stupid things, growing up, and him and his sister were never close because she was so much older than him. By the time he was in school, she got married and moved away. She has a daughter just six years younger than Paul. I told him how I didn't really have a family, just my mother. I told him about my dad leaving when I was young, about my mother's large family that I didn't know and have only met one time, both of my grandparents are deceased, and as far as my dad's family, I haven't a clue."

It was nice just to talk to Paul and be with him.

"So are you in a hurry to get home?" he said.

"No, not really."

"Let's take a ride then."

"Okay."

So when we got back to our hometown, Paul drove around and showed me where he grew up, the house he used to live in as a kid. It turned out we went to the same school. He was in high school. I was in junior high, and if we would have ever seen each other, he would have never noticed me. No one did.

"I loved school, or I should say I loved the sports part," he said.

"What sports did you play?"

"Football mostly. Yeah, it was a lot of fun. I also dated the head cheerleader, but she was too much into her looks for me, and I got sick of dating her and her makeup. When we were together, she was either putting on makeup or brushing her hair. Drove me nuts, and she was to skinny. Something I don't like on a woman. If I ever get married, I want two kids. I also want them close in age, not far apart like my sister and I."

"That's nice. I love kids. I haven't been around a lot of kids," I said.

"Yeah, I can't wait to start a family," he said.

"Neither can I."

"But I do want to wait a few years after we are married because I want to enjoy my wife for a while. You know, do things together, travel before we start a family."

I think at that moment if Paul would have asked me to marry him, I would say yes…oh yes.

"In my driveway," I said to Paul. "Would you like to come in for a while, maybe watch a movie?"

"I was hoping you would ask."

The next two hours, we sat on the couch, not touching and watched a movie. Then he got up and said good night. Maybe it was me, maybe he didn't feel attracted to me. Paul always left me feeling very confused.

Chapter 13

The next evening, Paul was at my house at 6:00 p.m. sharp. I could tell he was a little nervous about meeting my parents. This was the first time I had ever brought a guy home to meet my mother, so I was just as nervous as Paul. But, of course, this was the first thing for a lot of things for me.

Right away, they made Paul feel at ease. Right after dinner, Bill took him outside to show him some trees he had planted.

"I would love to build Dana a bench with a flower bed around it. She loves yellow roses. I want her to be able to sit and enjoy her flowers, when I talk her into retiring that is," Bill was telling Paul.

"Well, just let me know when you want to get it stated. I know about building."

"Oh, that's right, Tina told us you were in construction."

I helped mom clean up the dishes, then we went outside to join the men. We stood on the deck and watched as Bill talked a mile a minute. Every once in a while, Paul would look my way with those beautiful eyes. He was so handsome. I wanted to be with him every minute of the day. Paul walked up to me and did something I was not expecting. He put his arm around me, and I almost melted. The first time he ever touched me, other than on the dance floor, it had to be in front of my parents? I knew they saw the many colors of reds that were on my face. But after that, I wasn't aware of anything around me but his arm. It felt so wonderful, and I didn't want him to ever remove it.

But he did remove it, and he took my hand.

"Thank you so much, Dana, for a great meal. You are an awesome cook," Paul said.

Mom looked so pleased. "Well, thank you for coming. It was very nice to meet you, and we will be expecting to see a lot of you, I hope," Dana said.

"Oh yes, you will," Paul said and gave her a hug. "And let me know, Bill, when you are ready to build that bench and garden."

"Yes, sir, I will," Bill said as he shook Paul's hand.

Paul held my hand all the way to the car, then he opened my door for me.

On the way, neither of us spoke. At my house, Paul walked me to my door and said good night.

"Would you like to come in for a while?" I said.

"No, thanks, I have a lot of things I need to get done, but I will call you tomorrow."

I tried not to show my disappointed as I told him good night. I saw Joan had called me a few times. I forgot to call her back a few days ago; I felt bad.

"Hey, Joan, sorry I didn't get back with you the other day, but I went out of town with Paul for the day."

For a second, Joan didn't say anything, so I kinda knew she was upset with me.

"Wow! Tina, you and Paul have been spending a lot of time together," she said.

"Yes, and I love it. So how have you been?" I asked.

"Like I need a friend." I could hear the sadness in Joan's voice.

"I'm here. What if I come pick you up? We can hang out just like we used to," I said.

"That sounds great, Tina."

So I went to Joan's and picked her up. We didn't say much until we got back to my house.

"So what have you been up to?" I asked.

"Well, I met a guy, and he is nothing like Tim."

"That's great," I said, not for sure if that was great, she was seeing a guy; or great, he was nothing like Tim.

"But there's something that is bothering me about him."

"What's that?" I said.

"Well, first of all, he won't go to the club with me."

"Well, Joan, you know there is more to life than the club."

"I know," she said, "but it's more than that. He calls me at work, and he tells me he wants to see me, but he always asked me if I can come to where he is, which is like forty miles from here at a hotel. That's where he is staying right now because he is having his house remodeled. And haft the time, I can't go because my mother won't let me use her car, and I'm scared I'm going to lose him."

I knew I was taking a chance by asking Joan this because I didn't want her to be upset with me, but I had to ask.

"Joan, do you think maybe he is married?"

Joan didn't look to shocked by my question. She just said, "I don't think so, but it makes sense because he doesn't want to take me to the movies or out to eat just his hotel room."

"Joan, you need to get away from him. I mean I didn't like Tim, and he was a jerk, but he wasn't married."

"Well, actually he was," she said.

"What? he was married, and you knew this?"

"Not at first, I didn't. But I look at it like this, if they are happily married, they wouldn't be with me."

"Well, I look at it like this, they are jerks! And you are too good to be with jerks!"

"Yeah, Tina, it's easy for you to say that. You have Paul."

"If I wasn't seeing Paul, I still wouldn't date a married man. And if I was to find out Paul was married, I would kick him to the curve so fast… Joan, do you want to be a home-wrecker?"

"I don't want to talk about this anymore. I thought you would understand."

"I do understand, Joan. I understand you are lonely, and you feel like you have to take the only man that pays attention to you. But that's not true, you are a very pretty girl with a big heart. You do not have to settle with someone that is already taken. You deserve better than that."

"I know you are right, Tina."

I dropped the conversation. "Okay, let's have some fudge."

Joan decided to spend the night.

The next morning, when I got up, I heard Joan in the bathroom talking on her cellphone.

"Hey, Tina, what time can you take me home?" she yelled through the bathroom door. When she came out, I answered to her, "As soon as I get dressed. Is everything okay?"

"Yeah, a girl called off today at work, and they want me to come in."

Joan was quite on the way to her house, like something was bothering her.

"See you later, and maybe we can do something this weekend."

"Sounds great," she said, "bye and thanks for having me over."

Chapter 14

I went back home, cleaned my house, washed my hair, and laid my clothes out I would be wearing if Paul calls, but Paul didn't call. So at 11:00 p.m., I went to bed with a broken heart.

My phone woke me. I looked at the clock; it was 2:00 a.m. Who would be calling me at this hour?

"Hello?"

"Hi, Tina, It's Paul. Sorry to be calling you at this hour, but I want to know if I can come over?"

"Right now? What's wrong, Paul?"

"Nothing. I just need to be with you, Tina."

Any other time that would have been music to my ears. But right now, I was still upset he hadn't called me when he said he would.

"Okay," I told him, "when are you coming?"

He said he was on his way, so I got dress at lighting speed. Just as I was finishing my makeup, I heard him knock at my door. I had so many butterflies and wonders, like why now he wanted to be with me?

"Tina, I'm so sorry. I know it's late, but I needed to tell you something."

"It's okay, Paul, come in."

Just inside the door, Paul took me in his arms and kissed me. "I have been wanting to do that for weeks," he said.

"Wow, I have been wanting you to do that for weeks," I said. "If you have been wanting to do that for weeks, then what has stopped stop you?"

"You have," he said.

"Me? Paul, I was starting to think you weren't attracted to me."

"Are you kidding? You are beautiful, but I was scared. You have to understand, Tina, my wife did a number on me, and I can never go through that again."

"But, Paul, I'm not your wife. I would never hurt you, never."

Paul stayed a long time, and we talked. But this time, we talked about our future together. I knew one day, I would become his wife. After he left, I went back to bed but couldn't sleep. Replaying every word, life was good.

Joan showed up at my door right after I got up. I felt like I had a hangover, and I had a headache.

"Hey, Joan, come in. What's up?"

"Tina, I need a big favor from you."

"Okay." I could tell she had been crying; her face was red, and her eyes were all swollen.

"Last night, I spent the night with Mark, and my mom found out. She got so mad at me. She said if I stay out all night one more time, I have to move out of her house."

"Sorry, but you know my feelings about you seeing a married man."

"I know how you feel, Tina, but please stop judging me and be my friend. Mark has asked me to go away with him for the weekend, and with or without your help, Tina, I'm going. I love Mark, and I can't help it. And if my mom calls you, I need you to tell her I'm spending the weekend with you. I already told her that. So I know she will be calling you."

"Joan, we are not kids anymore."

"I know, but I can't move out of her house. I have no place to go right now."

"What weekend?"

"Next weekend," Joan said.

I didn't want to lie to her mother, but I didn't want to lose Joan's friendship, so I told her I would. I felt like we were teenagers lying to our parents. The thing is, I never had a friend as a teenager and never had to lie. But if I did, I'm sure this was how it felt. But Joan is my friend, even if I didn't agree with her seeing a married man, she already knew how I felt. I just hoped her mom wouldn't call. After Joan left, I was making coffee when Paul called.

"Good morning, are you awake?"

I loved hearing his voice. "Yes, I am, and good morning to you."

"Tina, again I'm so sorry about last night."

"You mean this morning?" I said with a laugh. "It's okay. I'm glad you came over. It made me feel better about us."

"Me too. I feel like we got a lot of things straighten out."

"So what would you like to do today? Spend it with me, I hope," he said.

"I would love to spend the day with you, Paul."

"Okay, I will be there in an hour if that's okay?"

"That's fine. I will be ready."

It was nice to have a boyfriend.

This time, when Paul picked me up, he came in and gave me a kiss. We had a good time, went out to eat, went to the zoo, and after we got back to my place. Paul came in; we watched a movie, and then talked. It felt so right being with him. That night, I went to bed with hope.

Chapter 15

I had a hard time at work the next day. I couldn't concentrate on my work, and I kept making mistakes. I was just so happy. I couldn't get Paul off my mind; I was so in love.

Becky, the other girl in the office, came up to my desk. "Tina, Bill has been trying to call you. He said your phone is off because it goes to your voice mail. He needs you to call him right away."

At once, my heart felt why was he calling me? Was something wrong with Mom?

Bill answered on the first ring.

"Bill, what's wrong?" I said.

"Tina, I'm on my way to the hospital. They just called me and said they think she may have suffered a light heart attack."

"I'm on my way, Bill."

I almost ran out the door; the tears were already falling, and I couldn't seem to stop them. I knew I had to get a hold of myself. I knew she hadn't been feeling good. I just thought she was wearing out from all the hours she has put in at work.

The drive only took ten minutes, but it seemed like an hour. I know Bill had said it'd been a light heart attack, but it was a heart attack that was all that kept going through my head. Everything went through my head on the drive there. She said she hadn't been feeling good, but she said it was from lack of sleep from working so many hours.

When I got to the hospital, I went to the nurse's station and gave her Mother's name. She pointed down the hall. She said the doctor was with her right now. She asked me if I was her daughter.

When I told her I was, she told me I could go in. As I walked in, the doctor was talking to Bill.

I went and put my arms arounds her. She looked good, just tired, and she had a tube in her nose

"Tina, I'm so sorry to cause so much worry, but I'm fine," Mom said.

When the doctor left the room, I asked Bill what he has said.

"The doctor said it was very mild heart attack, but they want to keep her overnight and run some more tests. He wants her to slow down and get more rest. If everything looks okay with the tests, she can go home tomorrow."

Mother took my hand. "Tina, don't worry about me. I will do as the doctor tells me. I promise."

Bill took my mom's hand and told her, "Yes, you will because you are quitting your job!"

"Honey, I don't want to go into this again. The doctor didn't say I had to quit my job. He said to slow down, and I will."

"Mom, please listen to your husband," I begged her.

"You guys, please stop worrying about me. I will be fine," she said, but I wasn't believing her, and neither was Bill that she would slow down.

"Bill, you can go home. I will stay the night with Mother."

"No, you both go home. I will be okay. I will just sleep anyway," Mom said.

"Hello."

I turned to see Paul standing there holding flowers.

"Hi, come in. How did you know?"

"I called the office, and Becky told me, so I came right over." He gave me a kiss on the cheek and walked over to Mom's bed. "These are for you. I know you like yellow roses."

"Oh, Paul, they are beautiful. Thank you, and yes, I love yellow roses. So sweet of you."

Paul walked over to me and put his arm around me. "Are you okay?"

"Yes, thank you for coming."

"So what did the doctor say?" Paul asked Bill, so Bill told him everything that he had told me.

Mother waved Paul over. "Paul, will you do me a favor please?"

"I will do anything for you, Dana."

"Please make my daughter go home."

Paul walks over to me. "You heard your mother. You have to go home. She is strong, and she is going to be okay."

And then Bill told me he was staying with her and promised to call me if there were any changes.

So after kissing her goodbye, Paul walked me to my car.

The next day, she did come home, and I went there to visit with her. I had to listen to her and Bill arguing about her quitting her job. I hoped he would win, but I knew how stubborn my mother could be, but she did agree to take some time off. I guess that was better than nothing.

I stayed for a while and made them lunch. The house was already spotless, so I told her I would be back after work tomorrow. I called Joan and told her about Mother. She asked if she could come with me tomorrow to see her.

"Yes, that would be great. I'm sure she would love to see you."

I think my mom is already bored. She has to be doing something at all times.

Bill took a vacation to stay with her this week.

Chapter 16

Paul came over, and he brought pizza. "Tina, make no plans for Saturday."

"Okay, why?"

"I'm not telling you."

"Paul, you know that's going to drive me crazy, just tell me."

"No." Then he dragged me off the couch and started tickling me.

After work I picked Joan up, not really wanting to know, I asked Joan how it was going with Mark.

"Oh, Tina, it's going great. I'm so happy, and I asked him if he was married, he said yes. But they weren't happy, isn't that great?"

I just looked at her like she was crazy. "Joan, then why is he still with her?"

"He won't be for long. I know he loves me too."

I was happy we pulled in at Mom's because I knew I wouldn't be able to keep my mouth closed.

"Mom, you look so much better. See, just a few days off work, and you look better."

"Well, I must admit… I do feel better. Come on, girls, I want to show off what my husband is building for me. It is so pretty."

We went outside. Bill was working on the bench and the flower bed for Mother and was almost done. It was beautiful. I hadn't seen so many yellow roses in my life. It was breathtaking. There were little bird houses and butterflies everywhere.

"Oh, Mom, I would so quit my job and sat out here and enjoy this every day."

"I know that is what I have been trying to get her to do."

There was a beautiful bench seating in the middle of flower beds that went all around it with just a little opening, and it was very big, not closed in. He put bird houses and butterfly houses every so far apart. He had nothing but yellow roses in all the flower beds. There were two big trees, so there were lots of shade. It was so pretty.

"Bill, how did you get this done in one day?" I asked.

"Well, thanks to Paul. He came over early this morning with all the building material, and we got it done."

I know; my mouth fell open. "What?"

He didn't say anything to me about this.

"That was so sweet."

"Yes, it was. I could have not done this by myself. The man knows his business."

I made Paul supper. I wanted everything to be perfect, including myself for tonight. When Paul arrived, he brought me flowers and a bottle of wine. He was so cute. I could just sit there and look at him all day. I gave him a big kiss. "Thank you so much for what you did for Bill and Mom today. That was so kind and sweet of you."

After we ate, Paul helped me clean up the dishes, and he fell asleep on my couch. I sat there looking at him. I often asked myself, *why me?* He could have any girl he wanted. I've seen the girls look at him at the club. I knew I was the luckiest girl alive.

The next day, I went to Mom's and cleaned her house while she followed me around, saying, "Tina, I'm okay. You don't have to come over every day. I'm not a child."

But I just kept on cleaning, she wasn't winning this one.

After visiting for a while, I went home to get ready for my date with Paul and his big surprise. Paul took me to a nice restaurant. I felt very out of place there. After we were seated, the waiter brought us a bottle of wine; he poured it for us. Paul looked at me and smiled.

"What is up with you, Paul?"

"You are," he said, still smiling. "Tina, I love you very much, and these last few months have made me so happy. I want to spend the rest of my life with you." Then he came over and knelt down. "Tina, will you marry me?" He put a beautiful ring on my finger.

The last few days, when I thought about what his surprise was going to be, this never entered my mind. I thought this would be years down the road.

"Yes, yes, I will." Tears running down my face, I know I looked a mess, but I was so shocked. "I love you so much, Paul." I went into his arms, and everyone started clapping. "Paul, can we do something?"

"Anything you want."

"Let's get out of here before they bring us the menus please."

After paying for the wine, we went to pizza place. I will remember this night for the rest of my life—the happiest night of my life.

The next morning, I got dressed and went to Mom's after a sleepless night. I had to tell someone. When I walked in, Mom was lying on the couch.

"Mom, I have some news I want to share with you and Bill. Is he around?"

"He's outside working in the garden. What's up?"

"Let me get Bill first." After I got Bill in the house, he had to wash his hands. He was taking a long time, and I thought I would go crazy with this held in news. At last, Bill came and sat by Mom.

"Okay, what's this big news?" Bill asked.

"Last night, Paul asked me to marry him." I just blurted the words; nothing like I rehearsed on the way over here.

Bill gave me a hug. Mom started crying. Everything I expected from them.

"Oh, honey, I am so happy for you. Paul is a great guy."

"I know he is, Mom, I am so happy."

"Hey, let's go upstairs, and you can try on my wedding dress."

I remembered Mom's wedding dress. It was beautiful, and I knew I wanted that dress to be the one. "Oh, Mom, are you sure?"

"Yes, I'm sure. Every mother wants their daughter to wear their wedding dress."

We went upstairs, but to both of our disappointment, the dress was to small. I would have to diet a very long time to get into it, and I didn't want to wait that long to marry Paul.

"Don't worry," Mom assured me, "you will find the perfect dress just for you."

We went back downstairs. Mom fixed us lunch, and we talked about the wedding.

"So have you guys set a date yet?"

"No, not yet, Mom, we just got engaged last night."

"I know I'm just so excited."

"As soon as we do, you will be the first to know." I hugged them goodbye and went home.

Paul was coming over soon, and I hoped we could set a date and talk about the wedding.

After we ate, we sat on the couch, and before I could say anything, Paul said, "Okay, how about June 11. It's on a Saturday, and I can put in for my vacation, so I can take you on a honeymoon."

"Wow, okay, June 11 is fine with me." I ran into the kitchen and got the calendar off the wall. "That's only two months away. Are you sure we can get everything done that soon?"

"Well, another thing, Tina, I don't want to have a big wedding, just a few friends and family if that's okay with you, and I thought we could have a small reception at the place we met, the club."

"Wow, Paul, sounds like you already have everything planned."

"Only if everything is okay with you. I stayed up all night thinking about everything. I can't wait until you become my wife. I love you so much, Tina."

If Paul only knew he could have asked me to get married at the city dump, I would have said yes. All I wanted was to be his wife, and nothing else mattered. I still couldn't believe he was even dating me, much less wanting to marry me. I felt like I was in a dream.

We spent the day together talking about our future, our plans. We would live here in my house for the first few years, then Paul wanted to build our house. We both wanted two kids or maybe three. Paul told me he didn't want his wife to work but to be a stay-at-home mom. He said he didn't want another person raising our kids. I just sat and listened to him, fulfilling my every dream.

Chapter 17

I called Mom from work the next day.

"Oh, Tina, I have been waiting for your call. So did you two set a date?"

"Yes, we did, June 11."

"Oh, great, next June. That will give us time."

"No, Mom, this year."

"Tina, not this June!"

"Yes, Mom, this June."

"Oh my goodness, this is April. That's only two months away."

I could hear the wheels turning in my mother's head. "Mom, we are not going to have a big wedding. Paul and I talked about it last night. We already know what we want, just a small ceremony with a few friends and our families, and Paul wants to have the reception at the club."

"At the club!"

"Yes, Mom, he thought it would be nice to have it there since that is the place we met, and I agree."

"Okay, well, can we at least rent it for the reception."

"That would be nice. I will talk to Paul."

"Mom, you have to promise me, you will not get carried away about this wedding and remember what the doctor told you about taking it easy."

"I promise. Don't you worry about me. I plan on being around for my grandchildren."

"I know, I can't wait to have a baby. Okay, back to the reason I called you, I wanted to know if Saturday is good for you to go with me to find my dress."

"Yes, that sounds great. I can't wait to see you in a wedding dress. I'm so happy. Life is so good."

Laughing at my mom's enthusiasm and eagerness, I think she was just as happy as I was.

"Okay, see you Saturday. I will pick you up at 10:00 a.m. I love you."

"Love you too, honey."

Next, I called Joan. She was working, so I told her to call me when she got home. I didn't want to share my news with her when she's working.

That night, Joan called me. "Hey, what's up?"

"I wanted to ask you something," I said.

"Okay, what?"

"Would you like to go shopping Saturday with Mother and I?"

"Oh, I would love to, but I would have to be back before six o'clock because I have plans with Mark."

"Okay, I will have you back before then."

"Okay, see you Saturday. What time?"

"I will pick you up 9:45 a.m."

The next day, Paul called me at work. "Hey, babe, I have some bad news. I have to go out of town to check out a job. I will leave today, and I won't be home until late Sunday night."

"Oh, Paul, I hate that. That's almost a week."

"Yeah, I know, but it can't be helped. It's my job, but I'm glad you will miss me."

"I will miss you like crazy. Joan, my mom, and I are going shopping for my dress, Saturday."

"Oh, that sounds like fun. Can't wait to see you in it. Did you tell your mom our plans?"

"Yeah, I did. I think she was a little disappointed about not having a big wedding, but she will be okay. I told her it was what we both wanted."

"Good. Okay, darling, I got to get off of here and go pack. I will call you tonight from the hotel. I love you."

"I love you, Paul, be careful. Bye."

The week went by so slow, but finally Saturday was here, and I was on my way to pick up Joan. I couldn't wait to see the look on her face when I told her what we were shopping for.

When Joan didn't come out, I went and knocked on her door. As soon as she opened the door, I knew something was wrong; her eyes were all red from crying. She grabbed her bag and almost pushed me out the door. When we got to the car, I said, "Joan, what is wrong with you? Why are you acting this way?"

"Sorry, I didn't want my mom to see that I have been crying. She would have asked me a million questions."

After we got in the car, I looked at her and said, "Do you think your mother was going to ask you the same questions I'm about to ask you?"

"Tina, it's nothing, I just had a fight with Mark."

"You want to talk about it?"

"What is there to talk about? He broke up with me, told me not to ever call him again. He said he would never leave his wife for me."

"I'm so sorry, Joan, but you will meet someone soon that is not married."

"Not everyone is as lucky as you are, Tina, to meet a Paul."

"I am very lucky, and I have something to tell you and ask you."

"What?"

"Paul asked me to marry him. I said yes, and I asked you to go shopping with mother and I today to help me choose my wedding dress and also ask you to please be my maid of honor."

"Oh, Tina, I'm so happy for you, and yes, I will be your maid of honor. Thank you for asking me. This is so what I need today—a little happiness."

Chapter 18

At the wedding shop, there were so many dresses. I knew it was going to be hard to choose, but I did find the dress. It was simple but very elegant. It wasn't the wedding dress of my dreams—that would have been Mother's wedding dress—but this one was very pretty, and since I wasn't having a church wedding, this one was prefect. We finished everything that day.

Joan and Mother found their dresses. We went to the flower shop. I ordered my flowers. We found our shoes. The last stop was the bakery where I ordered our cake. Mom and Bill said they would take care of the food for the reception, and a friend of Paul's was doing our pictures as his gift to us. The only thing left was reserving the club.

Paul and I decided not to go away for our honeymoon; we wanted to save for our new house, which was fine with me because the sooner we get our house, the sooner we can start our family.

The next night, as I was lying in Paul's arms on the couch, I asked, "How long do you think we should be married before we start our family?"

"Maybe a year or two, what do you think?"

"Paul, you know I want a baby right away."

He just laughed and held me tighter. I couldn't wait to become Paul's wife.

Joan and Mother gave me a bridal shower. There were only a few people there, but that was okay I was used to that. It was a lot of fun. I was walking on clouds. I had never been this happy and never wanted it to stop.

Chapter 19

The night before the wedding, Joan and I spend the night at mother's. The next morning, we went to the club to set everything up. It looked so pretty; everyone helped.

We went back to Mom's house, where we were to get ready. As Joan was curling my hair, I heard a knock at the door. A few minutes later, Mom came in carrying roses for me; they were from Paul. The note attached said, "You made me very happy. Thank you for becoming my wife today."

I couldn't help but cry. I loved him so much.

When we got to the park. where the ceremony was to take place, I was so shocked. It was beautiful; flowers everywhere, lights—I felt like a princess.

The ceremony went great, but I did cry during our vows, and I think I saw tears in Paul's eyes as well. Later, when we walked into the club, everyone cheered. I was now Mrs. Paul Sanford. How could it get better than this?

When Paul took me in his arms for our first dance as husband and wife, I knew it could get better. Every bad thing that had ever happened in my life was forgotten. When the night was over, and we were on our way home, for the first time, I got scared. What if Paul didn't like making love to me? I didn't want him to see me with my clothes off. But he put my mind right at ease, he turned the lights off and was very gentle with me.

Afterward, I lay in his arms, thinking that was it? That was lovemaking? I guess I read way too many books. All I felt was pain, a lot of pain, but I wouldn't let Paul know that.

I laid there long after listening to Paul's breathing. I didn't want to move out of his arms. I wanted to stay there forever, thinking how great it would to have Paul's child. We talked about it, and I knew he wanted to wait for two years, but I was ready now.

Sleep must have overtaken me because Paul woke me up making a lot of noise in the kitchen. I hadn't even heard him get up. After brushing my teeth and hair, I went into the kitchen to find Paul making breakfast still in his pj's. He was so cute.

Chapter 20

Monday morning came way too early for me. I wasn't ready to go back to work. It was going to be hard to stay away from Paul all day.

Right away, we started cutting back, not going out to eat but saving all we could to go toward our house and then maybe starting our family.

On weekends, we would go to Mom and Bill's for suppers, and sometimes they would come to our house. I didn't see a lot of Joan like I used to.

Life was good. I loved coming home and making my husband's supper and then lying in his arms watching TV. And then one day, Paul came home from work, looking kinda down. I could tell right away something was wrong.

"Tina, what do you think about taking a week off work and going with me to Virginia?"

"Virginia? Why?"

"Because I have to go there to oversee a new project."

"Oh, Paul, when?"

"We would have to leave in the morning."

"There is no way I can leave on such short notice."

"Yeah, I know, just thought I would give it a try, and I don't want to be away from you a whole week."

"I don't want you to either."

We just held each other for a while. I knew this was going to be hard, but I also knew this was just the first of us being separated. His job was always sending him away, but he got paid good when he had to travel for his job, and we needed the money for our house.

Friday, after work, I came home, feeling so sad knowing Paul wouldn't be coming home after work. I called Joan. She answered on the first ring.

"Wow, were you sitting on the phone?" I joked.

"Oh, hi, Tina. No, I had just hung up when it rang again. How are you? Haven't heard from in a while."

"Joan, I have tried to call you a dozen times. Didn't your mom tell you?"

"No, she never gives me my messages."

"Well, Paul had to go to Virginia for his job, and I thought I would see if you wanted to spend the weekend with me, of course, if you have no plans."

"That sounds like fun, just like old times."

Being with Joan did make the time go by faster. We spent the weekend shopping—rather she shopped, I just went with; I didn't want to spend money—then we talked a lot, got caught up on our lives.

Joan told me all about her new unmarried boyfriend. I was so happy for her. Paul called me every night. But the week still went by so slow, I didn't think Friday would ever get here.

After work, I rushed home to make Paul a nice meal. As soon as he walked in, I rushed into his arms. I missed him so much. After supper, I let him rest while I did dishes. He had looked so tired. These trips always took a lot out of him; he worked hard. When I came back into the living room, Paul was sleeping on the couch. I covered him with a blanket and went into our bedroom so I wouldn't wake him. I read a book until I fell asleep.

Paul was up and gone to work when I got up the next morning. Around noon, Paul called me at work. "Hi, stranger, how are you? Sorry about last night."

"That's okay. I knew you were worn out from your trip. I still love you."

"You better because I love you more every day, and I'm all rested up now."

I just finished setting the table when I heard Paul's truck, but then I heard him talking to someone. I looked out the kitchen window to see it was Joan. What is she doing here?

Today, of all days, I just wanted to be with my husband. Oh well, maybe she won't stay long.

"Hey, Joan, what's up?"

"Hi, Tina, I didn't have to work tonight, so I wanted to know if you want to go see a movie?"

"Oh, that is sweet of you, but Paul just got home last night, so I kinda want to spend some time with him. You understand, don't you?"

"Oh yeah, no problem. Don't worry about it."

And then Paul invited her to eat supper with us. I just knew right after supper, she would leave, but she didn't. After supper, she helped me do dishes, even though I kept telling her she didn't have to. Then right after that, she sat down and started watching TV with Paul, so I saw she wasn't in a hurry to leave. So I sat next to Paul and put my head on his shoulder, hoping she would get the hint, we wanted to be alone, but no. After three hours, Paul got up and said he was going to bed, that he had to get up early. So after he kissed me good night and told Joan good night, I just knew she would leave, but she just looked up at Paul and said good night and went right back to watching TV. When the movie was over, she went home, and of course, when I at last got into bed, Paul was fast asleep.

The next day, when I got home from work, Joan was sitting in my drive way. Well, this wasn't going to be a repeat from last night.

"Hi, Tina."

"Hi, Joan. Joan, you know, we love having you over, but tonight is not a good night. Since Paul got back from his trip, we haven't had any time alone, so I hope you understand."

"Oh, of course, I understand. I'm sorry about last night. I should have known."

"It's okay, don't worry about it. Maybe we can do something Friday night. Maybe the three of us or even the four of us could go out to dinner or something. I would love to meet your guy."

"Yeah, that sounds great. I will ask him."

After I gave her a hug, she left.

Chapter 21

Spending time with Paul, just the two of us, was so great. I had all of his attention. But that was short-lived when the phone rang. It was Paul's boss telling him once again he had to go out of town. I couldn't believe this. He had just gotten back, and I could tell by the expression on his face, Paul wasn't too happy about this either. I told myself I wasn't going to give him a hard time but try to encourage him.

So after he got off the phone, he told me it was just for the weekend.

"Paul, it will be okay. We have the rest of our lives to be together. Everything will be okay."

"You sound like you want me to go," he joked.

I put my arms around him and kissed him and let him know he was very much mistaken.

The next morning, I was late for work. I got up and made Paul breakfast before he left. As he was eating, I had to ask him, "Paul, do we have to wait two years before we start a family?"

"Tina, when I get back, we will talk about it, okay?"

"Okay, honey, I love you so much."

"I love you too."

After he left, and I was on my way to work, I couldn't help but smile, just to think this time next year, I could have a baby.

Joan was gone all weekend with her boyfriend. Mom wasn't feeling well. So on Saturday, I went and cleaned her house, fixed them dinner, and came back home. I was so bored. I called my aunt

Judy; I haven't spoken to her since Mom's wedding, but she did say I could call her.

I asked her questions about Mom growing up, and I was shocked at all she had to tell me. We talked a long time, and Aunt Judy told me things I couldn't even imaging about my mom. I already knew they were all raised in church, and I knew that her dad, my grandpa, was a pastor; my grandma was a Sunday school teacher; and Mom and her siblings all sung in the choir. My uncle Rob had told me all of this the same day I met him, but what I didn't know was that is where my mom met my dad. She said everyone believed he only came to church to be with her, and I could believe that because I could never see my dad in church; he was so mean.

When my mom was sixteen, it's when he started coming. He was a lot older than her, and she told me my grandpa was fit to be tied, and he wouldn't let my dad near my mom. But Aunt Judy told me Mom feel in love with my dad, and Mom and Aunt Judy shared a room, so Aunt Judy was the only one who knew what was going on. At night, Mom would sneak out and meet him. "I didn't like it," Aunt Judy said, "but she was my sister."

"So what happened?"

"Tina, I think your mom should tell you the rest. I think I have already told you more than I should have."

"Oh, please Aunt Judy. I promise I will not tell anyone what we have talked about today, and we both know Mom is never going to tell me anything."

Chapter 22

"Well, I see no harm in telling you some things, but you must promise not to repeat this."

"I promise."

"At night, when everyone was sleeping, your dad would come for her, and at daybreak, he would bring her back. This went on for about three months. I was so scared Father was going to catch her. It was hard for me to sleep.

Then one morning, after she came home, she went into the bathroom, and I could hear her crying. The bathroom was across the hall from our two brother's room, so I knew they were going to hear her. I knew your dad must have broken up with her, and I was glad. But when she came back to our room, it was just the opposite. That's when she told me she was pregnant with you.

"And she told me she was running away with him. The very next night that they were leaving town, she knew our father would kill her if he knew, and she told me she didn't want to cause her family shame. So we both cried and held each other for the longest time. You see, Dana was my sister but also my best friend.

"The next night, after she left with your dad, I walked the floor. I didn't know what to do. I knew our parents would ask me where she was, and I knew I had to tell them. I begged your mom not to go, but she was so set into it. Nothing was going to change her mind.

"Well, my brothers did hear, and they waited and followed them. My bothers never said, but your mom called me a few days later and told me, our brothers beat him and tried to force her to come home, but she would not.

"I know the police were never called because he was a lot older than Dana. She was only sixteen, and I guess he didn't want to go to jail or face my father. Dana kept in touch with me after I promised her I would never tell anyone where she was. She told me your dad told her she could never see her family again.

"When our father got sick, I called her, but she was so ashamed at what she did. She wouldn't come home. The same when Mother passed away. I don't think Dana has ever forgiven herself. It was just a few years ago, she started talking to the rest of the family."

"So that is why she never went back home?"

"Yes, Tina, I know your mom regrets what she did by staying away, and I think now she is trying to make up for it. She also told me that having you has filled that hole in her heart. Tina, you are your mother's world, and she has never, for one moment, been sorry she had you."

"Aunt Judy, I have asked my mom before why she never had more kids. She just said it wasn't in the cards for her."

"Tina, I have already told you so much I may as well tell you the rest."

"Your mom was six months pregnant when she lost the baby. I think you were like two years old. One night, your dad came home drunk and got into it with your mom and knocked her over the couch. Two days later, she lost the baby."

"My mom has never told me anything about her past. Now I think I understand why. Thank you so much, Aunt Judy, for telling me."

"I think she never told you because she was too ashamed. It broke everyone's heart when she didn't come home for both our parents when they passed, but all is forgiven now. And I'm just so happy to have my sister and you back in my life."

After we hung up, I just sat there thinking about everything she told me. No wonder Mom never talked about her family, what a heavy burden she carried all these years.

The next morning, Paul called me to tell me he was now getting on the plane and would be home soon. He sounded happy; I hope it was because he was coming home to me.

When I heard his truck in the drive, I almost ran outside and in to his arms. I never knew I could love someone this much. That night, I just lay there and watched Paul sleep and thought about our future together and how lucky I was and how thankful I was to have met the greatest man in the world—Paul was my life.

On our sixth month anniversary, Paul took me out to eat, and then we went to the club. It was fun to hang out with Joan and her boyfriend. He seemed nice, a little too flirty with the other women there, but Joan didn't seem to notice. I think maybe because she had a little too much to drink, so had I, so we left early.

At home, I went into bathroom to get dressed for bed when I heard the phone ring and Paul talking to someone. I walked in the bedroom, and Paul handed me the phone. It was Joan; he informed me.

She was crying so hard I could hardly understand her. She said Joe (her boyfriend) had left the club with a women, and she had no way home.

"Oh, Joan, I'm so sorry."

"Tina, please come get me. I have to get out of here, and I can't call my mom. I have no one else to call."

"It's okay, Joan, you have me and Paul. I will send Paul to come take you home, okay? It's going to be okay, stop crying."

"Thank you, Tina."

I looked at Paul, who was already putting his shoes on. "I'm sorry, Paul, I would go, but I've had too much to drink to drive."

He came over and kissed me. "Like I would let you drive," he said as he walked out the door.

I tried to stay awake and wait for Paul to come home, but I guess it was the alcohol because I fell asleep.

The next thing I knew, Paul awoke me getting into bed, even though he was trying to be quiet. I looked at the clock on my night stand, and it said 4:09 a.m.

"Paul, are you just now getting back?"

"Yes, your friend is crazy drunk and crying her eyes out. She wouldn't get out of my truck because she was scared she would wake up her mom, so I had to sit there until she became sober enough to go in.

"Oh, Paul, I'm so sorry."

"It's okay. I just want to go to sleep. Good night."

I knew he was upset with me for volunteering him to go pick her up and take her home. We both slept late the next morning. When I got up, trying hard not to wake Paul, I went in the kitchen to make him a big breakfast, trying to make up for last night. But he seemed to have forgiven me, he came in the kitchen smiling and gave me a big hug and kiss. Everything was good again.

I was going to bring up the subject of starting a family again but thought I would wait awhile. Everything was going so good I didn't want to rock the boat. Besides I told myself Paul knows how much I want a baby. I was hoping he would bring it up.

Chapter 23

We hadn't heard from Joan in two weeks since the night Paul took her home. I called a few times but always went to her voice mail. I hoped she was okay.

Paul came home to let me know his job was sending him out of town. And this time, he wasn't sure how long it would take. He said he was hoping only a few days. He left early Saturday morning. Usually he would call me when his plane landed, but it had been hours, and he should have been there long before now, so I started to worry. I had called his cell repeatedly but no answer; it went to his voice mail.

Later I went into the laundry room to put a load of wash in. I always check his pockets because he was always leaving pins in his shirt pockets. But this time, he left his cell phone in the pocket, and the ringer was off. That's why I hadn't heard it ring all the times I called it. I knew he was mad when he discovered he forgot his phone, poor Paul. I couldn't do anything until he called me. I didn't know what hotel he was staying at.

I worried all night, and the next morning, when he still hadn't called. I was beside myself. I had to talk to someone, and I didn't want to worry Mom. I tried calling Joan, but her mom told me she was with her boyfriend, Mark, so I guess she went back with him.

At noon, Paul called me.

"Paul, why didn't you call me? I was so worried. You forgot your cell phone."

"Tina, calm down. I'm okay, and I know, I forgot my phone. It's been crazy here. This is the first free moment I've had to call you, so get off my back please."

I was so shocked and hurt. He has never spoken to me like that. "Paul, I'm sorry. I was just so scared because you always call me."

"Well, I'm okay, and I'm sorry also. This job is really taken a toll on me."

"I know you work so hard, and I'm really sorry I acted that way. What day will you be home?"

"Tomorrow evening as of right now. If it changes, I will call you. I have to go." He hung up without even saying goodbye, or that he loved me.

I needed to get out of the house. I called Joan again, hoping she was home. She answered the phone on the first ring.

"Hey, how have you been?"

"I have been good, Tina. It's good to hear from you. What's going on?"

"Just bored out of my mind and was wondering if you want to hang out? Paul is out of town again."

"I would, but I have a date. I'm sorry."

"Oh no, that's fine," I said, "have a good time, and we will get together soon."

After getting off the phone with Joan, I read until I feel asleep.

After work, Monday, Paul's truck was in the drive. I was surprised he hadn't called me at work to let me know he was home but was so happy he was.

When I walked in, he was watching TV.

"Hey, sweetie," I said, giving him a hug. "When did you get home?"

"About an hour ago."

"Are you hungry? Can I fix you something to eat?"

"No, thanks. I have already eaten, just want to sit here and relax."

I sat down beside him and put my head on his shoulder, but he seemed not to notice I was there. I knew when he got home from trips, he was tired, but I needed him to hold me.

"Okay, I'm going to go take a hot bath, then if you're sure you don't need anything—"

"No, I'm fine."

I went into the bathroom and took a hot bubble bath, leaving the door open, just in case Paul wanted to join me. But after a little while, when he didn't come to check on me, I called for him.

He came and stood at the door. "Did you need something, Tina?"

"Yes, I was thinking you could join me."

His reply was, "Tina, you know I hate baths," and he went back into the living room.

I put on a sexy nightie and went into the living room just to discover he wasn't there. Looking out the window, I saw his truck wasn't there. What is going on? After changing into jeans and a shirt, I tried calling his cell. He didn't answer.

I blamed myself. I knew how his job has been a strain on him, and here I was trying to talk him into having a baby, when I knew he wasn't ready. No wonder he didn't want to have sex with me.

He didn't come home all night. I was so worried, I called, I cried, and I was so confused. But all I could do was wait. When he gets home, I will tell him I will wait until he is ready to start a family. I stayed up all night, waiting. I didn't go to work, but I knew I couldn't just sit here doing nothing. I needed someone to talk to, or I was going to go crazy. I called Joan, and she came right over. I told Joan everything. She held me while I cried and reassured me everything was going to be okay; I just needed to give him time. I hoped she was right. I knew Paul loved me but still worried I was running him off.

After we talked, I did feel better. And then Joan became very quiet.

"Joan, I'm sorry for doing all the talking about me. I feel like there is something going on with you. Do you want to talk about it?"

After a few minutes, she looked at me with tears in her eyes. "Tina, I'm pregnant."

I was so shocked.

"Joan, are you sure?" was all I could say.

"Yes, I'm sure."

"Well, what about the father? What does he say?"

"He is happy."

"Joan, that is great. Are you happy about it?"

"I want to be. He wants to marry me. He says he loves me."

"Oh, Joan, it will be okay. I'm so happy for you."

After Joan left, I couldn't help but feel a little jealous. I really thought Paul would be home by now. Where was he?

Chapter 24

The next morning, when Paul still hadn't return, I called into work and told them I was sick, and then I drove to Paul's work and talked to his boss, which confused me even more. What he told me made no sense. He told me Paul was on vacation and had been for almost a week.

Thinking he had him mistaken with someone else, I told him that was impossible. Paul had just got back from a job in Missouri.

"Look, I don't know what is going on with Paul lately, but I do know it's none of my business. You asked me about Paul, and I told you he's on vacation," and he turned and walked away.

Another sleepless night, but I knew I had to go to work, I couldn't lose my job. Right after work, I hurried home, hoping he was there or a message from him, but there was nothing. I needed someone to talk to. I couldn't go to Mom because I didn't want to upset her, and every time I called Joan, all I got was her voice mail. I couldn't sleep. My mind was going everywhere. What if he was hurt? Was he with another woman?

I got up and started going though Paul's things, looking for something, anything that might tell me where he was. I finally fell asleep in the wee hours of the morning from exhaustion. Paul woke me up when I heard him unlocking the front door. I just laid there. I didn't know what to say to him, so I waited for him, and after a while, he came into the bedroom and very quietly, he got into bed, trying not to wake me. Are you cheating on me? The words were out of my mouth before I knew it.

I think I scared him because he jumped.

"No! And I dare you to ask me that question." He almost shouted at me, but I didn't care if he was mad because I was mad, and I wanted some answers, and I wanted them now.

"I went to your boss, Paul. He told me about your vacation. Where have you been, Paul? You didn't go to Missouri on a job! Where were you?"

"Look, Tina, we just need some time apart."

"Some time apart? Are you kidding me? No, Paul, we need some time together." This time, it was me screaming. "Time apart is all we have had since we got married." The tears started falling as hard as I tried not to cry. "We have been apart and look at us. You need to tell me what's going on, and you need to do that now."

"Okay fine. You want to know? Then I will tell you. Yes, I have someone else, and I want to be with her! Happy now? I want a divorce."

I felt like my heart was going to explode. Even though I knew deep down he had to be seeing someone, there was still that hope that I was wrong. But to hear him say the words made it real.

"Why did you marry me? Why did you tell me you loved me?" I was crying so hard I couldn't talk. He just stood there looking at me like he hated me.

"I did love you, but that has changed."

"How can you love me one day and not the next?"

"It just happens. I don't know why or how, but it did, and all I know is I want out." With that, he turned and started packing his things.

"Paul, please, we can work this out. I know we can."

"No, Tina, I don't love you, and I don't want to be with you."

After he left, I don't know how long I stood there with my mouth hanging open. My marriage was over before it even started. I went to bed, pulled the covers over my head. I was sure I would die of a broken heart. I cried until there was no more tears.

The knocking on the door awoke me the next morning,

I opened the door to see Joan standing there crying with her arms open, and I went into them.

"Oh, Tina, I ran into Paul, and he told me. I'm so very sorry."

I didn't think I had any tears left.

"You've got to know we didn't mean to hurt you, and we never intended to get pregnant."

I pulled away from her. "Joan, what are you talking about?"

"Paul and I, we didn't mean to hurt you. It just happened."

"What just happened?" I demanded.

"We feel in love."

"Joan, are you telling me you and Paul have been seeing each other?"

"Yes, but we didn't mean to hurt you. Tina, I love you. I would never hurt you."

"And you thought sleeping with my husband wouldn't hurt me. Your mother is right about you. You are crazy. Get out of my house now, you psycho!" I pushed her out the door and slammed the door in her face. I called Paul's cell, but he didn't answer. I knew he wouldn't, so I left a message.

"Paul, you are a pig! Joan, of all people, you both are sick and deserve each other!"

My husband and best friend. I went back to bed and prayed sleep would take me out of this torment I was in. Even after all this I knew now, I still didn't want to lose Paul. If he only knew how much I loved him. He didn't belong with Joan; he belonged with me. The baby she was carrying should be our baby.

Sometime in the night, the tears stopped, and it was light outside, and then waking again, and it was dark again. For some reason, I felt safe. I didn't want to face life without Paul.

Chapter 25

When had all this happened? How long had she been sleeping with my husband? Was it when we were all three together? I just wanted answers. I wanted to know why.

At daybreak, I made myself get up and shower. I called in work and told them I was sick.

All day, I called Paul's cell but no answer. I even called Joan's cell, but she wouldn't answer. I just needed them to tell me why and when this happened. I needed answers. So I decided if they wouldn't talk to me on the phone, they were going to talk to me face-to-face.

I dressed and drove to Joan's house. Her mother gave me the address where they were staying. She kept saying how sorry she was. I found the address with no problems. This was by no means a big town, and I have lived here my whole life.

It was a division, where they were building new houses, and there, packed in a drive way, was Paul's truck. They must have been planning this for a while. If they have already bought a new house, this was my house, my husband, my family, and Joan stole that away from me.

I got out of my car and marched right up to the door. Joan came to the door. As soon as she saw me, she called for Paul and walked away. So I let myself in, the place was empty, which surprised me. I was sure it would have already been fully furnished, but the only thing I saw was a coffee pot and two cups.

Paul came out of a room; I was sure it was a bedroom.

"What do you want?" he asked in a very mean tone, not the loving Paul I knew, but this Paul acted like he hated me.

"I want some answers from you and Joan, so please call her back in here. I'm not leaving without someone talking to me."

"Why can't you just leave this alone, Tina, and go on with your life?"

"You came into my life and said you loved me, married me, and then left with my best friend, and the only thing you can say to me, is let it go!"

"Fine. You want answers? I will give you answers, then I want you out of my life."

At that point, I wasn't sure anymore if I still wanted answers. All I heard was Paul saying he wanted me out of his life. I didn't want the tears to come. I wanted to be strong. I didn't want them to see how weak I really was.

When Joan came back into the room, I could see she had been crying, and I was glad. She told Paul she didn't want to do this, but he told her in that loving voice that he was used with me so many times that it will be okay.

Paul started, "In the beginning, I thought I was in love with you, Tina, I really did. I didn't start out to hurt you. One night, I got up to watch TV because I couldn't sleep. Well, Joan called. She was at a bar, and she was very upset and wanted you to come pick her up because the guy she was with left her. I told her you were sleeping, but I would come and take her home, so I did.

"When I got to the bar, I tried to calm her down, and what can I say, one thing lead to the other. She was hurt, and I was lonely. We both agreed it would never happen again, but it was an agreement I couldn't keep.

"I told you I went to Missouri because I wanted to be with Joan. But the truth was, I have been here all the time. We didn't mean to have a baby this soon, that just happened, but we will be married as soon as you and I are divorced. Now anymore questions?"

All the time Paul was talking, Joan stood with her head down. I couldn't walk away without saying something to her. "Joan, take a look at me because one day, it will be you standing here. He doesn't love you. He doesn't even know what love is. And when that day comes, don't call me. Don't ever call me again."

I got in my car and drove to my bank without one tear falling from my eyes. Now I knew… I took everything out of our savings and closed the account.

The next morning, I made myself go to work. I didn't want to see or talk to anyone, but I knew I couldn't lose my job.

Chapter 26

Bill stopped by my desk around ten.

"Hey, Tina, have you talked to your mom this morning?"

"No, I haven't. Why?"

"Oh, just wondering, she hasn't answered her phone, so I going to run home on lunch. I'm sure she is sitting outside. Sometimes she forgets to take her cell with her." He sounded worried.

"Okay, if I hear from her before then, I will let you know."

Around noon, my supervisor came to my desk. I thought I was in trouble for missing so many days of work. I was not prepared for what he said to me.

"Tina, Bill called, and he is on his way to the hospital. They took your mom there, and if it's okay with you, I would like to drive you there."

"Oh my god, not again. Did Bill say how she is?"

As we walked out of the office, my heart was beating a thousand miles a minutes. I was so scared. When we arrived, Mom was still in the ER. Bill came out of the room with two nurses.

I ran to him. "How is she?"

"I don't know yet. The doctor is in with her now. They made me come out, just then the two nurses took us down to a private room and said the doctor would be in soon."

"Bill, how was she when you went home?"

"Tina, she was passed out in the kitchen. I couldn't wake her. I called 911. They just got her here a few minutes before you did."

Just then, we heard people running past the door. Bill looked out the door, and when he turned around, I saw tears in his eyes.

Only a few minutes had passed, but it seems like forever when a doctor walked in.

"Your mom has suffered a heart attack. We have called in a specialist. At this point, that is all I can tell you. You can see her in a few minutes."

Chapter 27

When we entered her room, I fought to hold back the tears. She was lying there so small. They had all kinds of tubes hooked up to her. I knew this time was different from the last time. I went to her and took her hand. I told her we were there, and everything was going to be okay.

The nurse came in and told us the specialist was there, and we had to leave. We went back in the small room when I saw Bill had Mother's purse. I took it and found Aunt Judy's number and called her after telling what had happened. She said she was on her way. I told Bill, and then the two doctors came in to talk to us. "Your mom has suffered a massive heart attack. There is nothing we can do but make her as comfortable as we can."

"Is my mother dying?" I asked the doctor.

"Yes," is all he said.

I ran out of the room and into my mother's room. I put my arms around her and begged her not to leave me. Bill was there crying. He told my mom to hold on; her sister, Judy, was on her way. He took her in his arms, tubes and all, and kept saying, "I love you so much, my darling, please don't go."

So many things were going through my mind. It was like nothing was real. It was just a bad nightmare, and I was going to wake up. I was frozen. I couldn't move from where I was standing. I just watched as Bill held her and talked to her. Then he held out his hand to me. I took it and laid my head on my mom for the last time. I told her I loved her, and then she was gone.

I had to get out of there; I couldn't breathe. A nurse lead me into another room sat down with me. Another nurse came and gave me a glass of water. Then a man came in and started talking to me about God and asked if he could pray with me. I remember shaking my head yes.

Bill came into the room, and we held each other and cried. I kept hearing the same words over and over: it's going to be okay. Bill took my hand and said, "Let's go."

I didn't ask him where. I just let him lead me. I felt like a lost little girl. We went back to Bill and Mom's house. I didn't want to go in, so we sat on the front porch, neither of us speaking. After a while Bill told me Aunt Judy and my other aunts and uncles were on the way, but it would take several hours to get here.

"Bill, can you please take me to the plant to get my car? I need to go home." A fresh wave of tears fell down my face.

Back at home, I just lay on the couch. I knew I should stay with Bill, but I just couldn't go into that house with my mother not there. For the first time in a long time, I prayed for God to give me understanding of why this was all happening. I must have fallen asleep.

The next morning, Bill called me to tell me my family was here, so I dressed and went to Bill's house. As soon as I saw Aunt Judy, I just broke down again. She looked so much like Mom. She held me for a long time. I was so happy all these kind people I didn't really know were here. But I did know I needed them, and so did Bill. They stepped in and took care of everything. We were so grateful because I knew I could not make arrangements to put my mother away.

Chapter 28

When the doorbell rang, and Uncle Rob opened it. I was shocked to see Paul standing there. He looked at me and held out his arms to me, and I went into them. He held me while I cried more tears, then Aunt Judy asked him to please take me upstairs and make me lie down.

He led me upstairs and laid down with me, but sleep was far from me. It felt so good to have this little bit of comfort. I knew then that Paul and I would be able to work this all out. I knew he loved me, and I loved him, so we could fix this.

I lay in his arms, hearing him breathing. I could tell he fell asleep, so I turned and kissed him on the cheek. He jumped up so fast; it scared me.

"What's wrong?" I asked.

"Oh, Tina, when I heard about your mom, Joan asked me to come over here and help you through this ordeal. I told her this was a bad idea. I knew you would get the wrong impression, but we were so worried about you. Joan loves you so much, Tina."

"Are you kidding me? Yeah, she loves me so much that she slept with my husband. You or Joan have no clue what love is." I got up and walked to the bedroom door and opened it. I knew at that moment, I never wanted to see Paul again. It was truly over. "Goodbye, Paul."

He walked out the door and out of my life without a word. I didn't go downstairs until I was sure Paul was gone. My uncles were seated at the table, talking. They told me Bill and my aunts went to make the arrangements. I went home and took a long bath. I just wanted to be alone. I wanted to dig a hole and crawl into it and pull the earth in after me. So much hurt was inside of me. I didn't think I could stand it.

When I got out of my bath, I noticed my answering machine had three messages on it. The first was from a girl at work, telling me how sorry she was and how much she would miss my mother. The next one was from my boss telling me the same. But the last one took my breath away...when I heard my mother's beautiful voice. "Hey, babe, it's Mom, just wanted to touch base with you. Haven't heard from you in a while. How is everything? I've been working in my garden all morning. My yellow roses are just beautiful. You should come by and see them, and also, I'm bored. Come keep me company. Ha-ha. Okay, talk to you soon. Love you."

Then the phone went dead.

Where was I when she called? Oh, Mom, I miss you so much. How was I going to live without her?

I laid on the couch and cried myself to sleep. The knocking at my door awoke me; it was my aunts. They went around taking care of business as if they lived here. Aunt Sue put on a pot of coffee and made me breakfast, even though I'm sure the food was good; it felt like cardboard in my mouth. I did eat a little just to please them.

We sat around while Aunt Judy told stories about Mom when they were growing up. It made feel close to my mom.

"When Dana was fourteen, and I was thirteen, there was a boy in school that I was head over heels in love with. So one night, I told Dana about him, and she talked me into calling him. At first, I said no way. I was too scared, but your mom had a way to talk me into anything. So shaking, I dialed his number. But as soon as someone answered the phone, I freaked out and threw the phone to Dana. I will never forget the look on her face, but she pulled it off. They talked for a while while I was hiding my head under the pillow. She told him how great I was and how I really liked him. He told her he liked me too. We became boyfriend and girlfriend for about a week until I found out he was a jerk.

"Dana and I always had so much fun, until your dad came along. Then she changed; she wasn't the happy, laughing-all-the-time girl. She had so many dreams before he came into her life. We used to stay up late talking about those dreams. She wanted to be a teacher and marry; she wanted four kids, two boys and two girls. She loved kids. She wanted to learn the piano. Dana had a beautiful voice."

My aunt's eyes got all teary. I had never heard my mom sing, not even in the shower. It was like she was talking about a stranger. What if these people had not come to Mom's wedding? I would have never met them, and I would have no family at all. I would be all alone in the world. That was a scary feeling. But thank God, they did come, and they were here now.

Chapter 29

If my mom had not met my dad, how different her life could have been, and maybe her dreams would have come true. I know my dreams turned into nightmares. I wanted so much to be Paul's wife and to have children.

"Well, I think it's time we get started back to Bill's house. We have a lot to do tomorrow," my aunt stated.

"Tina, will you please come with us. We don't want to leave you alone."

"No, I will be fine."

"I'm staying here with her. I already told Rob, so you guys go ahead," my aunt Judy said.

I was glad Aunt Judy was going to stay with me, even though I would have never asked her to stay. I had so many questions to ask her, but we only stayed up a little while after the others left. I knew she was tired, so I didn't ask any questions. I did hope there would be time to talk before she went back home.

The next morning was cloudy and raining, just like I felt inside. I cried so much last night; I awoke with a bad headache. After we dressed, we drove to Bill's. Either of us saying few words; I could feel Aunt Judy's pain as I'm sure she could feel mine.

The visitation at the funeral home for the family wasn't until three, so we sat around and talked, or I sat and listened as they told stories about Mom growing up. There were laughter followed by tears. I had no idea how we were going to get through the next two days, or how I was going to get though the rest of my life once my family left.

My uncle Rob was going to preach the funeral tomorrow. Other than that, I didn't know much my aunts had taken care of all the details. My mom had a small life insurance. I was very thankful they stepped in and took over

Bill didn't seem to be in a state of mind to handle anything, and I knew I wasn't. Bill's house had so much food from very kind people. It seemed like every hour, someone was bringing in a covered dish and sympathize words—mostly from everyone from the plant where we all three worked.

If only Mom could be here to see all the kindness of her friends and coworkers, but she would never know. My aunts got busy cleaning the house and putting away food while I went upstairs to lie down until it was time to go to the funeral home.

All I could do was lay there thinking that in one week I lost my best friend, my husband, and my precious mother, I just wanted to wake up from this nightmare. Before I knew it, Aunt Judy tapped on my door.

"Tina, we will be leaving soon, thought you might want to freshen up."

"Thanks, Aunt Judy, I'll be right down."

How was I going to be able to see my mom in a casket?

I wanted to pull the covers over my head and stay there forever.

Chapter 30

As we walked into the funeral home, there were so many family members already there. I remember seeing a lot of them at the wedding, but for many, this was the first time meeting them. I didn't know I had so many cousins.

There were so many flowers; I was overwhelmed. Then I looked to the front and saw a casket surrounded by even more flowers, and I knew I was going to have to walk up there and see my mother.

Both my aunts took each arm and asked me if I was ready.

My aunt said, "She looks so good, Tina, and no more pain. She is at rest."

I knew those words were to make me feel better, but they were not working. My heart felt like it was being torn from my body. The tears immediately started to fall as we started to walk. I just kept thinking I can't do this. I can't do this.

When we got to the casket, and I looked down at my mother's sweet face. She looked so small. I just wanted to hold her, to take her home; she didn't belong here.

Bill came up and put his arm around me. I could see so much hurt in his face. He loved my mom so very much. His brother stood close to him. I was glad he was there for Bill.

When visitation was over, we walked outside. The rain had let up some. It was sad to know Mom would never walk outside again, never sit in her garden again looking at her yellow flowers. With that thought, a fresh wave of tears came. It was so unfair; she was the only one I had, and now she is gone. She would never hold me again. I would never hear her laugh again. I felt like I didn't belong anywhere. I felt so lost.

There were a lot of people at the funeral, and everyone was so kind. I didn't go to the grave site; I couldn't stand to see them put her in the ground, so Aunt Judy took me home. I was so glad Aunt Judy was here with me, but I knew soon everyone would have to leave and go back to their own lives. I hugged her and told her I would miss her when she went back home and how I appreciated everything she and everyone has done.

"Tina, the rest of your family and I have been talking about you coming back home with us. Your uncle Rob could use your help in his office. He is always so overwhelmed with paperwork. He was going to hire someone anyway, plus you would be with family you could get to know cousins you don't know. There is nothing here for you. Please say yes, you can live with me and Uncle Rob for as long as you want."

She was talking so fast I couldn't really comprehend all she was saying.

"But what about my house?"

"We already discussed that with Bill. He said he would sell it for you."

"Aunt Judy, I appreciate everything you are trying to do for me, but this is my home. My job is here, my house. I don't think I can just leave it."

"But why? You asked me why your mother stayed? Why are you staying? Everything you had is gone, Tina, don't put your life on hold. Live it now while you have it. Come with us, be around your family. Let us help you."

Chapter 31

"I promise I will think on this. It's just so new right now. I never considered ever leaving here, so I need to think about it, and right now, I'm not sure my mind can make a decision like this."

"Okay, honey, don't think about it right now, just get some rest. We will talk more in the morning."

"Aunt Judy, you don't have to stay here with me. You should go be with your husband. I will be fine."

"No, I'm staying right here. You aunts will be here soon enough, so you should rest for a little while. They are bringing us food, so don't worry about supper."

I gave her a hug and went to my room. I lay there staring up at the ceiling. I knew my aunt was right—there was nothing here for me. I also knew if I stayed, there was the chance I would run into Joan and my Paul, and I don't think I could stand that.

For some reason, I felt like if I left here, I would be leaving my mom. But I also thought I can't go back to work at the plant where she worked every day. I knew every day my heart would break over and over. Maybe I did need a new start. I know Bill will get on with his life; he did have a lot of family here. What was keeping me here was just heartache. I know the heartache wouldn't leave me, but maybe by starting new somewhere else, where there was not so much memory. Maybe this was exactly what I needed.

Sleep must have overtaken me because the next thing I knew, it was dark outside, and I could hear low talking coming from the living room.

"Well, hello, I hope you got some sleep."

"Yes, I did, thank you, and also I thought about what you asked me, Aunt Judy, and I have decided to give it a try if the offer still stands."

"Absolutely!" my aunt Judy said as she gave me a big hug, as did all my aunts. They seemed very happy about my decision.

"Okay, first thing in the morning, we will pack everything up," Bill said.

"He will sell for you what you don't want to keep and store in his garage what you do want to keep. Your uncle Rob said he will rent a U-haul to take whatever you want to take, and Bill said he will put the house up for sale."

"Well, it all sounds great, but I don't want to put anyone out."

"Don't you worry about putting anyone out, your family wants to help."

So early the next morning, they showed up and started getting busy. I had a great family and didn't have the heart to tell them just how scared I was, and that I had changed my mind a thousand times last night, so I just said… "You all have done so much already."

"This will help us also. We won't have to worry about you being so far away from us, but you will be right there for us to look after. That's what family is for," my aunt Lisa said.

I wish Mom was here to give me answers on what to do. She had been my only friend my whole life, the one I talked to about everything. I never got the chance to talk to her about Paul and I because of her health. I didn't want to worry her; she never knew what Paul and Joan did to me, and I was thankful.

As I was taking things out of a cabinet above the refrigerator, I saw an envelope sticking out from under some old canning jars. It looked like a letter. Tears filled my eyes as I saw mother's beautiful handwriting. It was addressed to Lisa Freeman. I opened it, and it read…

> Dear Lisa,
>
> I miss you so very much. I wish over and over I was there with you, with my family, because I know that is where Tina and I belong, not here.

> I wish things was different, but they are not, and I'm scared they will never be. Maybe one day, I will be able to face my sisters and brothers again, but not now. I'm so sorry for everything I have put my folks through, and now I will never be able to tell them just how truly sorry I really am.
>
> Love you, xoxoxo
>
> Your sis, Dana.

Why hadn't she mailed this? I took it to Aunt Lisa.

"Aunt Lisa, I found this, and I'm sorry I opened it."

She took it in her hand and looked at it for a long time. Then she sat down and began to read it; tears fell down her face. When she was done, she stood up and hugged me.

"I would have been so happy to receive this letter from her. I waited every day to hear from her."

"I can't understand why she didn't mail it, but, Aunt Lisa, this letter gave me peace by leaving here. I needed to find this to know what my mom would have done if she could have."

"And that, my dear Tina, is why she didn't mail it."

We held each other and cried then went back to work. I knew for the first time, I was doing the right thing, and it gave me hope. I felt like it was her way of saying I needed to be with her family—my family.

I stood at the doorway of the only home I have ever known. It was empty now with only memories left inside.

Chapter 32

The car was packed and waiting for me to start over hundreds of miles away, but I wasn't worried anymore.

My aunt Judy drove my car. I guess she didn't think I should be driving. As I sat and looked out the window, I felt like my life was passing by as fast as the trees on the side of the road. Just two weeks ago, I was home with my husband talking about starting our family with my mom living less than ten miles away. I had a great friend, a good job—how could so much change in such a short time. I could feel the hot tears running down my face. If only I had a crystal ball to tell me what's in store for my life.

It seemed to take forever to get to Aunt Judy and Uncle Rob's house. When we arrived, it was dark, so I couldn't see the house. Uncle Rob told us to go inside; he would unload the car in the morning, which was okay with me. I just wanted sleep, so I took my overnight bag and went inside. It was a big beautiful house. Aunt Judy showed me my room.

I unpacked my overnight bag, took a hot bath, got into bed, and didn't even turn over until morning. I awoke to the smell of bacon cooking, and I realized just how hungry I was.

Over breakfast, Aunt Judy told me she had lived in this house since her and Uncle Rob had married. They raised two kids here. She had a son in the air force, and a daughter who lived right down the road; her and her husband had twin girls age six—Sandra and Sara her only grandkids, who she adored, and cousins I had never met.

After helping Aunt Judy clean up, I went back to my room to unpack everything my uncle had placed in my room. I loved the walk-in closet; her home felt so warm and welcoming. After everything was put in place, I went back down stairs to find Aunt Judy sitting out by the pool.

"All done? If there is anything you need, dear, just let us know. We want you to feel at home here."

"Oh, thank you, Aunt Judy. Yes, everything is great. I'm so glad I came."

"I'm so glad also. I hope it's not too much on you, but Rachel and the girls will be over soon. They can't wait to meet you."

"That's fine. I can't wait to meet them."

I sat down beside my aunt while she went to get us drinks, and it just hit me out of nowhere. I wasn't home, and Mom was gone, and as much as I tried not to cry, the tears came again. I was glad when my aunt came back out with Rachel and two darling-looking girls.

"Hi, I'm Rachel, your cousin. I'm so happy to meet you." She hugged me, as well as both girls.

"This is Sandra and Sara," Aunt Judy introduced us.

"Hi, I'm so happy to meet you."

"Aunt Judy, you have a beautiful daughter and beautiful granddaughters."

"Yes, I do," Aunt Judy said with a big smile.

Rachel laughed a lot. I could tell she was very happy and so was the girls, even though I'm not their aunt. They started calling me Aunt Tina, which was fine with me. I changed and played in the pool with them. I never thought I would smile this much again, but they made me happy. I just knew Rachel and I could be friends. She was so outgoing and happy.

Aunt Judy made us lunch. We stayed in the pool a long time because it was so hot today. Rachel and I talked; it took a lot off my mind today, and the little girls made me so happy. She told me she had married her high school sweetheart; they had been married two years before they had the twins. They were both so happy when they found out they were having twins.

I loved spending time with Rachel and the girls. Lying in bed that night, I wondered if I would ever find love—I mean real love. I wanted a family so bad. Again I cried myself to sleep, missing my mom, just thinking about all she had missed out on being with this loving family, and all I had missed out on our lives could have been so different.

Chapter 33

The next morning, Uncle Rob told me to take some time for myself before starting the job, but I felt the sooner the better. I wanted to start saving to get my own place. Later that day, I was excited when Aunt Judy asked if I would like to take a walk and stop by Rachel's for a visit.

The neighborhood was so pretty, and as soon as Rachel opened the door, Sara and Sandra almost jumped in my arms. These little darlings knew what my heart needed.

While Aunt Judy visited with her daughter, the girls showed me their rooms and all their toys. It was a great day, and I was sorry when it was time to leave.

On Saturday, Rachel and her family came for dinner, and I got to meet Mike. He gave me a big hug like he had always known me—another great day. Even though I missed Mom like crazy, every day was getting easier for me.

Aunt Judy and Uncle Rob's son, Kevin, was coming home for a visit, so there was a big family cookout. I met cousins for the first time, a lot of second cousins, and Kevin was sweet and charming, just like I knew he would be. He was two years older than Rachel. I could tell they were very close.

Everyone was so sweet to me—what a great family—they went out of their way to make me feel like I was a part of them. How could Mom walk away from this for my dad, which I wondered if he knew that she had passed or even cared.

My first day at work went well. Everything seemed easy enough, mostly what I did before: answer phones, set up appointments, and a lot of bookkeeping. Aunt Judy was right; Uncle Rob was so overloaded, so it was gonna take a while to catch everything up, but I was so ready to do. It put my mind on work instead of missing Mom and thinking about Paul.

Since there was only a few people working here, right away I felt at ease, and I just knew I was going to like it here. I wanted to do my best; Uncle Rob was so kind to give me a job and a place to live. I wanted to please him, so I worked very hard getting everything in the office cleaned and organized.

At the end of the week, I had everything looking so much better, and a filing system that made sense, and I could tell Uncle Rob was pleased. At home, he kept bragging to Aunt Judy about me being a godsend—that made me feel good.

Chapter 34

Rachel and Mike was always inviting me to their house for supper or to the movies. Sometimes I went, and sometimes I would babysit, so they could go have some time together without the girls. I looked forward to those times when I would put the girls in bed and read them stories. I would pretend they were mine, and this was my little family.

Every day after work, I was always off doing something with someone. I had no time to be sad, but at night, when I was alone, I cried in my pillow and talked to my mother. I was getting used to everything now, my new surroundings and my new family. But I needed to get my own place, I didn't want to wear out my welcome here. I was saving every dollar I could to get an apartment or something.

I was so happy when Bill called and told me the house was sold. That was money that could go toward my new home. Aunt Judy wouldn't let me pay anything to stay here. I had tried many times, but they wouldn't hear of it. They made me feel like their daughter—a very good feeling.

One Saturday afternoon, I was lying on the couch, reading, while my aunt and uncle were out when the phone rang. Answering it, I was surprised to hear Mike on the other end. Rachel called me a lot but never Mike.

"Hi, Tina, it's Mike. What are you doing tonight?"

Hoping he was going to ask me to babysit, I said nothing.

"How about going to a movie and dinner with us?"

"Oh…" Hoping I didn't sound disappointed, I said sure.

"Who is watching the girls?"

"My cousin has them for the night. Can you be here around 7:00 p.m., or should we pick you up?"

"Oh no, I will come there, and seven is fine."

At 7:00 p.m., I was at their door, but before I had a chance to ring the doorbell, Rachel opened the door, looking gorgeous as always. She had a big smile on her face, and I knew this was not just a movie and dinner kinda night like so many times before. Something was up, and I didn't think I wanted to know what.

But here he was, this good-looking guy. I could only assume he was to be my date for tonight. I almost felt sorry for him as I did for myself, thinking he was put into this not by his choice. But really I know they meant well, but what were they thinking? This guy was so far out of my league. They had to be kidding, and I'm sure he was now thinking the same thing.

"Tina, this is Scott, my very best friend in the world besides Rachel, of course." They both laughed, and it sounded like Mike had already started drinking.

"Hi, Tina, very nice to meet you." he said, extending his hand to me.

"It's nice to meet you, Scott."

Thankful at that moment, Mike put a drink in my hand. I had a feeling I was going to need it to get through this night. Three drinks later, we left for the restaurant. Thank goodness, Rachel drove. Mike and Scott rode in the back. I had never seen Mike laugh so much. Apparently he was having a very good time. They both laughed and joked. They had Rachel and I laughing. Maybe tonight wouldn't be so bad after all.

At the restaurant, it was different. I didn't know what to say, so I just sat and listened to the conversation going around the table by the three of them, hoping it would be over soon, and we could go to the movies, where at least it would be dark, and I wouldn't have to talk.

Scott sat next to me at the movies, and I could smell his after-shave and right away, I thought of Paul and how much I missed him.

When we left the movies and got into the car, Mike got in the front seat with Rachel, so I got into the back with Scott, which I didn't like because I didn't have anything to talk about. I also knew I would never see him again, so I just wanted this night to be over. But Scott didn't seem to have a problem finding something to talk about; he had a way to put me at ease.

When we got to Mike and Rachel's place, Scott asked if I would like to sit on the deck for a while and talk, and I said yes. He told me his wife died four years ago of cancer, and he has a five-year-old son, Scottie, which was his world. He said he came from a big family also, and right now him and Scottie were living with his mom because he wanted to buy a house. He had four sisters, all older than him and a younger brother. He has known Mike since they were kids.

Scott was so easy to talk to. I found myself telling him the reasons I came here—about my mother. I liked talking to Scott. I knew nothing could ever come from this, but tonight was nice. He walked me home. I was shocked when he asked me if he could call me sometimes.

After changing into my pj's, I lay in bed going over tonight, wishing I could change the way I acted. But even though we had a nice conversation, I really didn't expect to hear from Scott, and that was okay. I needed time for my heart to heal.

Scott called me at 8:00 a.m. I was still in bed, not asleep but lying there thinking about Mom—how I missed talking to her.

"Good morning, beautiful."

My heart fell to the floor. This couldn't be happening.

"Good morning, what are you doing up so early?" I asked.

"Couldn't sleep and was wondering if I could see you today if you don't have plans?"

"No plans," I said. I did want to see Scott even if it was just as friends. I wasn't ready to put my heart back on the chopping block just yet, even if his good morning was the best I had ever received. He was such a sweet person, and he was so easy to talk to.

I met Scott a little later at a café near a park. I had been there once before when Rachel and I took the girls there. After Scott and I had lunch, we walked in the park. Scott made me laugh; he was so fun to be around. I wondered if he was always like this. He talked a lot about his son. All four of his sisters lived close by. Three were married with kids—one was still at home, and his brother was away at collage. It sounded like a very close family. He said his mother insisted on Sunday dinners at her house. It was a wonderful afternoon, and I was sorry to see it end.

Chapter 35

When I got home, Aunt Judy told me Rachel wanted me to call her as soon as I returned; I already knew why.

"Hey, Rachel, you wanted me to call you?" I joked.

"Yes, so tell me…tell me… How was your day, and how long did you guys stay up last night, talking?"

I could hear the excitement in her voice. "Well, today was good. We went to lunch, and then a walk in the park. We talked, and last night, he walked me home around two in the morning, then he called me at 8:00 a.m."

"Oh, Tina, I'm so happy you two hit it off. Scott is such a sweet guy. He has been through so much. Mike and I are so fond of him. He is like family, and we both knew you two would be prefect for each other. When his wife was going though cancer, Scott stayed every minute by her side. He had a hard time after she passed. He just shut down. Last night, it felt so good to hear him laugh."

"Rachel, his wife passed away four years ago. He hasn't dated since then?"

"Yes, he did date a girl that was separated from her husband for about four months, but she ended up going back with her husband."

"Rachel, I think Scott right now is just looking for a friend, and so am I, and I love talking to him, but let's not get to carried away. Remember, we just met hours ago."

We both laughed.

"I know. You're right, of course, but if I could pick out his next girlfriend, it would be you."

"Well, thank you, cuz."

After I got off the phone, I thought about Scott. I felt like a guy like that could never be interested in me, and besides I was still in love with Paul. I knew Scott just wanted friendship, and I don't know if I felt relief or disappointment. I told my aunt and uncle I was looking for a house to buy. And I knew they truly didn't want me to move out. It made me feel good to know they wanted me to stay. I honestly didn't feel like I was ready to be on my own just yet.

Scott asked me out for Friday night. I was so excited, even though I knew I shouldn't be; we were just friends. I had to keep reminding myself I was still in love with Paul.

This time at the restaurant, I had lots to talk about. I told Scott all about Paul and Joan, and what had happened.

"Well, Paul, sounds like a pig."

I couldn't argue with that. I had wondered how long it would take Paul to put Joan through what he put me though.

After the movie, we went to Mike and Rachel. The girls were already in bed. We played cards until 3:00 a.m. When those three get together, they are so funny; I had never laughed so hard. Scott took me home, and he kissed me good night. It was a sweet kiss that lingered on my lips.

Monday morning, Rachel stopped by the office.

"So guess what?' she said.

"What?"

"A little bird told me that Scott was going to ask you to go to his mom's on Sunday to meet his family."

"What? Rachel, I don't want to meet his family right now. Scott and I are just friends. We just met!"

"Oh, it will be okay. It doesn't mean you have to marry him, but Mike tells me Scott really likes you."

"Seriously?"

"Yes, seriously, and why wouldn't he? Tina, you are great, even if you don't see that. You have so much to offer a guy. You are beautiful inside and out. Now let's go have lunch."

"Let me ask Uncle Rob if now is good."

"Now it's fine," Uncle Rob said as he came into the room, giving his daughter a big hug. "How's my little girl?"

"I'm good, daddy, can we bring you back anything?"

"No, thank you, I'm taking your mother to that new restaurant tonight."

On the drive to the café, my mind was going everywhere… Scott likes me… I had so many butterflies. I knew I couldn't eat any lunch today.

Scott did call me the next day and asked me about Sunday. I didn't dare tell him Rachel had already told me, so I agreed to go. He said he would pick me up at noon Sunday. I couldn't concentrate on my work all day. I couldn't come up with an excuse to get out of Sunday. I just knew I didn't want to go.

At home, Rachel called to say the girls wanted to come over for a swim, and I was glad; I needed to talk to Rachel. I took my coffee out on the back deck to wait for Rachel and the girls. Aunt Judy was baking cookies for us, and the whole kitchen smelled wonderful. She was singing "How Great Thou Art," and it brought tears to my eyes. I wondered if my mother's voice was as sweet as Aunt Judy's.

Sometimes when I got to missing Mom so much, I would call Bill, and we would talk about her. I also called just to check on him. I could always hear the sadness in his voice. I knew he loved my mother very much. The last time I talked to him, he told me he had all mother's things packed away for me whenever I was ready for them. Hearing the girls come up the driveway on their bikes broke me out of my thoughts. I went back into the kitchen just in time for hugs.

"Hey, Aunt Tina. Hey, Grandma."

"Hey, Sara. Hey, Sandra, how are my beautiful girls today?"

It was so nice to see Aunt Judy with her granddaughters. Then it was my turn for hugs. Rachel and I went out to the pool while Grandma gave the girls milk and cookies.

"Okay, what's up? You said you wanted to talk to me?"

"Oh, Rachel, I don't know what to do. I don't want to hurt Scott's feelings, but I don't want to meet his family right now. I don't even know Scott, and it's not like we are in a relationship. I'm still in love with my husband." Instantly I realized what I just said sounded so stupid.

"But I thought you and Paul were divorced now." Rachel looked worried.

"We are, we are, that was crazy. He is not my husband anymore. I just get so confused sometimes on where my life is headed. I'm so scared of starting a new relationship with anyone ever again because the hurt is so great. Rachel, will the pain ever go away?"

"In time, the pain will go away." She took me in her arms and let me cry. "Sweetie, you can't live your life afraid of getting hurt because that is a very lonely life, and you are too young to be alone for the rest of your life. You need a husband you can trust, and children you can love, and one day, you are going to be a great wife and mother. But not right now, it's not time for you to meet Scott's family, and he will understand. Tina, if you like Mike and I will talk to him, but please don't let Paul control your happiness. He has already taken so much from you. Don't give him anymore."

"No, I want to go. I'm going to take your advice, and I'm not giving Paul one more second of my life. Thank you so much, Rachel, you have no idea how much this talk has helped me."

"Oh, that makes me so happy, Tina, good for you, and, honey, I know you are not used to being around family, but Scott's family are so down to earth. You will love them, and they will love you. My family has known their family for years, but I have some great news for you. Well, I mean I hope it's great news anyway. Scott must have since your uneasiness about meeting his family, so he has invited Mike, me, and the girls over Sunday also."

"Oh, Rachel, that does make me feel more comfortable. Thank you." And I gave her a big hug. I already adored Rachel; she was the kindest person I have ever met, and I was so glad I came here and met my sweet cousin.

Just than my uncle came in the room, and after giving Rachel a hug, he asked to see me in his office, which was strange, but I followed him in, and after closing the door, he asked to be seated. I had never been in his home office before, but I could tell Aunt Judy had decorated it for him. It was very manly, but without a man's touch. Uncle Rob sounded very businesslike. I started getting a little worried.

"Tina, I know you want to buy a house and be on your own, but I just wanted you to know, your aunt Judy and I are very happy you are here. But if it is what you want, we will help you anyway we can."

"I thank you so very much, Uncle Rob. You and Aunt Judy have been so kind to me."

Chapter 36

Sunday, Scott picked me. Wearing jeans and a T-shirt, he looked like the kind of guy who walked around with a tall blond on his arm. I could never picture myself as Scott's girlfriend. Even though I knew Rachel would be there, I was still very nervous about meeting his family.

Scott kept reassuring me it would be okay, and they would love me. I had never met a guy's family before. I didn't know what to expect. When we pulled up, two of his sisters I assumed came up to the car before we could get out. Everyone made me feel very welcome.

Scott's mom gave me a hug and told me she was very happy I had come.

"Mom, where is Scottie?"

"He is in the house," his sister said.

"I'll be right back." Then Scott walked toward the house. A few minutes later, he came out holding the hand of a small boy, who looked just like his dad. It was love at first sight. This little boy was adorable.

I went to them and knelt down. "Hi, Scottie."

He buried his face into his dad's side.

"Scottie, this is Tina. Remember I told you about her."

He shook his head yes but still didn't look at me.

His little face lit up when Sara and Sandra came; all his shyness just went away. The girls gave me a hug, then the three went to play.

Rachel gave me a hug. "So how are you doing?"

"I'm okay. You're right, everyone is very nice."

When we all sat around to eat, I liked it when everyone held hands to pray, just like at Aunt Judy's house. There were a lot of conversation and laughter. After the meal, I helped clean up and got to talk to his sisters and play with kids; it was nice. His sister told me if I asked Scottie to see his trains, she was sure he would love that, so I did.

"Hi, Scottie I hear you have trains. I would love to see them."

He took my hand and led me inside to his room. I was shocked to see his room; it was beautiful. The train went all around the room; it was amazing. It had trees, bridges, train stations, and houses. I think I could have stayed there all day, playing with this train set and being with this little guy.

His dad and the twins came in.

"How's it going?"

"Dad, Tina likes the trains, but she don't know how to turn the lights on."

He seemed to think that was funny.

"Yeah, I love this set, and he's right, I couldn't find the light switch." I put my hand up, and Scott helped me up.

"Dad, can Tina come back and play with me?"

"We will have to ask Tina, son."

Scott looked at me and winked; my heart did a flip.

"I would love to, now that I know where the light switch is at."

"Okay, guys, grandma has ice cream waiting."

"Yay!" all three kids screamed at the same time and went running out.

"You have a great son."

"Yes, I know. He was just a baby when his mom died, so he don't remember her."

"It must have been so hard on you."

"It was, but I thank God for my family. They took over with Scottie when I wasn't able. I went into such a depression. I had missed so much work. I lost my house, but I didn't care because I didn't want to live there without Lori. But what I missed the most was my time with my son. Mike and Rachel were always there for me. They never gave up on me. They are like my family."

"Yeah, they are great people. I wish I would have been raised with them, all of my family."

"Well, you are here now."

Chapter 37

The next day at work, I would catch myself thinking about Scott. I knew way down deep that this was not good. I was only putting myself out there to get hurt again, even though I knew Scott was a nice guy, and I truly believed he would never intentionally hurt me. But I also knew a person can't have feelings for someone if those feelings were not there, and I had a feeling I would be the one with the feelings for Scott. But what if Scott couldn't return those feelings after a while, I would get hurt, and I don't want to get hurt again.

I remember Paul telling me he would never hurt me, and Paul has made it so hard for me to trust again. I hope in time I won't have these trust issues, but for now, I want to protect my heart. I have wondered if Paul and Joan have married, and did she have a boy or a girl? Are they happy?

Aunt Judy stopped by the office to have lunch with her husband. "Tina, I'm going shopping today for our cookout Saturday. Is there anything you need for the salad you are making?"

"No, Aunt, I have gotten everything already."

"Okay, have a good day, dear."

Aunt Judy and Uncle Rob were having another one of their cookouts for the family. It was always a big event. It seemed like family here were always having cookouts.

The week went by fast and before I knew it, I was in the kitchen with Aunt Judy and Rachel cooking. Rachel was always asking me questions about Scott. I knew her and Mike wanted us together—that was very obvious. But I told her if it happens, it happens.

"Okay, but did you invite him here today for the cookout?"

"Yes, him and Scottie will be here shortly."

Everyone started showing up, and the fun began. I always had fun when kids were around. All of these people were my family, how lucky was I? When Scott and Scottie showed up, he was one of the family—even Scottie was giving out hugs. I tried to keep busy and help out as much as I could, so Aunt Judy could visit. I was clearing off a table when I looked up and saw Scott smiling at me.

"What?"

"I think you are beautiful, that's all." And then he walked away.

I was in so much trouble. I could fall for this guy so fast. Scott was talking to Mike, so I went over and stood next to him. "Scottie seemed to be having a good time." I really didn't know how to bring up a conversation right then.

"Yeah, he loves being around the twins," Scott said with that beautiful smile. "Hey, let's go get drink, shall we?" And he took my hand and led me in the house.

"Okay, but the drinks are in the cooler by the pool."

"I know."

I just laughed and followed him. Just inside, he pulled me in his arms and kissed me.

"I have been wanting to do that since I got here." Scott always seemed so real; nothing phony about him, and I liked that.

Mike walked in, so I excused myself and went back out to help Uncle Rob. I had noticed when Mike and Scott were standing together, there was nothing but laughter, and everyone that walked up to them walked away laughing. Had I already started to develop feelings for Scott?

Everyone started getting in line for food. Mother's fixing their children's plate. I hoped one day that would be me. Scott sat with me after we got our plated. Scottie was seated at a table with the other kids.

"Would you like to go see a Disney movie tonight with Scottie and I?"

"I would love to." I think I said a little too excited.

Chapter 38

It turned out to be the best date I have ever had in my life; we ate popcorn, and we laughed. Scottie sat between us. When it would get a little dark in theater, Scottie would take my hand; it was so cute. He fell asleep on the drive back to my house. Before I got out of the car, Scott kissed me good night—what a prefect night.

Aunt Judy was lying on the couch when I came in.

"Hi, you looked so tired" I said.

"Yeah, I love having my family here, but it takes so much out of me. I will be fine after a good night's rest. Thank you for all your help. How was your date with the boys?"

"I had a great time."

"I know I haven't told you this because I didn't want to put my nose into your business, but we couldn't be happier that you and Scott are dating. A match made in heaven, I say."

"Well, thank you, Aunt. I do like him, but I'm a little worried about dating so soon, not sure I'm ready."

"I can understand that. Scott is like a son to me. I have known him since he was a little boy, and I know first off he's a great man and a great dad."

I reached down and kissed her on the cheek. "Get some rest. I love you, Aunt Judy."

"Good night, sweetheart."

I went to my room and called Rachel. "Hey, am I calling too late?"

"No, not at all. How was your date?"

"It was good."

"Sounds like you need to talk… I'm all ears."

"Well, I know you are probably getting sick of the same old talk, but I don't understand some things."

"Like what?"

"Like when I'm with Scott, sometimes I'm thinking about Paul and missing Paul, and what we had in the beginning, and I don't want to have these feelings, but I don't know how to get rid of them, and I know this is not fair to Scott."

"Tina, I don't think it is Paul you are missing. I think it's like you said you miss what you and Paul had. But the truth is, what you have told me about Paul, you didn't have anything but a pack of lies, and that is not love, and it is not a marriage, it's was only false hoping on your part. You want to be loved, and you want a family, but don't you see now you were never going to have that with Paul.

"But you are with someone now, that is real. He is not a fake like Paul was. Sweetie, you have to give yourself time. If you like being with Scott then be with him, even if you do miss Paul. That will end one day. But don't walk away from a great guy just because you still have feelings for a jerk.

"Just take one day at a time and don't try so hard to look in to the future because one day you will have that husband and children, and it will be so much better because it will be with someone that loves you."

I cried listening to Rachel talk. I knew she was right. "Thank you, cuz, for talking to me. As always I feel so much better."

"Good. Have a good night's sleep, and whenever you want to talk, I'm here for you… I love you."

I kept myself busy, and as far as Scott was concerned, I made up my mind: I wasn't going to worry about getting hurt anymore. I did find an apartment that was very nice and not far from my job and in my price range. I filled out the application. Scott and I talked every night on the phone. He told me his family really liked me, and he said Scottie kept asking when I'm coming back over.

Rachel called on Friday to ask if we wanted to come over for pizza and play cards. I told her I would ask Scott and get back with her. Scottie was also invited. It was a wonderful evening, playing cards, playing with kids. Scott and I played hide-and-seek with them. It was so much fun. He was a great dad. I really believed this evening was the changing point in my life; no more tears on my pillow. I was putting the past in the past where it belonged and getting on with my life.

"Hey, how about tomorrow night, I take you out on date with us two?" Scott asked as we were hiding.

"Sounds great."

The next day, I wanted to look my best for our date, but all my dressy clothes were too big for me, so I went shopping and had my hair and nails done. It felt good to pamper myself again. It had been so long since I had. And by Scott's expression, I knew it was worth it.

We went out to dinner and then dancing; he was a really good dancer, and then we just parked in front of Aunt Judy's and talked. We talked about our dreams; he wanted what I wanted, a home and family. I fell asleep with my head on his shoulder. I don't know how long we stayed there. When I woke, he was also sleeping. "Scott, wake up."

"What time is it?" he asked. "I'm sorry. What a great date, I am falling asleep on you."

"I fell asleep too," I said laughing.

"It is 5:00 a.m. I really never pictured our first night together would be like this." He joked.

"I kissed him. I will call you later." I got out of the car, hoping not to wake my aunt and uncle up.

The more Scott and I talked on the phone; the more I was falling in love with him.

Chapter 39

At work, Monday, Uncle Rob came into the office. "Hey, take your old uncle to lunch."

"Okay, where would you like to go?" I asked as I grabbed my purse.

We had a nice lunch; it was different. Uncle Rob talked about his church and about God. He was a dedicated pastor to his church. Some of the things he was telling me brought tears to my eyes. I thanked him for lunch. It was good to get to know him better, a side of him I didn't know. I was shocked when Scott called me that night and asked if I would go away with him for the weekend and even more shocked when I said yes.

"It's a little place in the country. I know you would love it. They have a lot of little shops. We can take a boat to a little island, have a picnic, rides bikes. It's beautiful there."

"Wow, Scott, it sounds beautiful, also sounds like you have been before."

"Before my dad passed away, the family would go there once a year. It's been a long time since I have been, but it is where I had a lot of good memories."

"I can't wait," I said.

"Okay, we will leave Friday after work if that works for you?"

"Sounds good."

I spend the rest of the week packing and repacking. I didn't know what to bring, so once again I asked for Rachel's help, who was more than willing to help. She was so excited when I told her. She told me to bring my suitcase and what I already had packed to her house, so I did.

We went through her clothes; she had so many beautiful things, some fit me, some did not, but we were able to put some things together that I was very comfortable with.

I was ready…

But after telling Aunt Judy I was going, I didn't get me the response I was hoping for. I thought she would be glad, but she wasn't.

"Tina, you know I can't condone you going away with a man that is not your husband."

"I know, Aunt Judy, but it's not like we will have the same room. But if it upsets you, I won't go."

"Child, I'm not upset at you. I just worry about you since my sister, your mom, passed away. I feel like you are my daughter, and this is what I would tell Rachel if it was her, no matter your age. It's because I love you. I hope you understand."

"I do understand, and I promise I will be careful and use my head."

"Okay, sweetie, that's all I ask," she said.

I never thought about why Scott asked me to go away with him, and if we would be sharing the same room. I guess I never thought of his intentions if he even had any. I wasn't going to start worrying about it now. I didn't want to live for the future, nor the past.

Friday, after work, I rushed home and took a shower. By the time I carried my suitcase down stairs, I set it outside on the walk-way, so Aunt Judy wouldn't see it. I didn't want to upset her again, then I walked into the kitchen, where I heard Scott and Aunt Judy talking.

After we drove out of the city limits, and the country came into view. It was so pretty. It was fall, and the leaves were turning colors.

"Oh, Scott, this is beautiful."

He started to laugh.

"What's so funny?"

"Honey, this is not what I was talking about, but if you like this, just wait until you see what awaits us."

When we arrived at the B&B, I became a little uneasy, but soon Scott put me at ease when he unlocked the door to my room. Why would I expect anything less of Scott? He was a gentleman. The room was adorable; everything looked homemade. After we freshened up, we went out to supper. It was walking distance to the restaurant. The scenery was beautiful just as Scott said it would be.

After our meal, we walked around, saw a lot of couples taking the same late-night walk, holding hands. My heart felt so light, so glad we came.

Back at our rooms, Scott asked if I wanted to come to his room and watch a movie or turn in for the night. I wasn't ready for bed, so we watched a movie. It felt so nice being in Scott's arms and feeling his lips on mine. I knew when it was time to go to my room.

The next morning, Scott called and woke me up. "Good morning, beautiful."

I loved his good morning. "Good morning."

"How about breakfast?"

"Sounds great, give me a haft an hour, and I will meet you downstairs."

"Okay."

I took a quick shower and got dressed. I was looking forward to spending the whole day with Scott. After we ate, we went to some little shops and took a boat to a little island. They sold already made-up baskets for picnics, but first, we rode bikes all around the island. After returning the bikes much later, we got our baskets and went to the lake to eat. It was so pretty and peaceful, watching the swans. I never knew a place even existed other than in the movies.

The day went by fast…too fast. Back at the B&B, Scott told to dress nice, but he wouldn't tell me where he was taking me. I was dressed and waiting for him outside his door. When he walked out, he had on black dress pants and a nice shirt with a tie. He looked great.

I wore a black dress and heels.

"You look gorgeous," he said.

He made me feel good. We went dancing and had a blast. We were slow dancing, and he was holding me tight, then he whispered in my ear. "I think I'm falling in love with you."

I knew right then the feelings I had with Paul was not love but only gratitude that he would love or say he loved me. I had never—not even by my own father—felt love by a man the way I felt it right now. I knew I just wanted Paul to love me because my whole life I had been put down by others because of my weight. But with Scott, it was so different, just like Rachel said it would be. This was true love… I could see myself spending the rest of my life with this man.

"Okay, I'm feeling very awkward right now. I hope those words didn't scare you, Tina."

"No, they didn't scare me. Those words thrilled me, Scott, because I know I'm falling in love with you."

Chapter 40

The next morning, we took another walk before leaving for home.

"Oh, Scott, I don't want to leave."

"I promise we will be come back soon, and maybe we can share the same room as husband and wife."

"What? Is that a proposal?"

He just grabbed me and swung me around. "My proposal will be much better than that."

"I should hope so."

Scott carried my bags inside Aunt Judy's house. I was glad it was Sunday, and they were in church. Scott held and kissed me like he didn't want to leave me, and I felt the same way. As soon as he left, I missed him.

Since no one was home, I did some cleaning and laundry. When my aunt and uncle got home, we had a nice visit. They told me all about church and how they wished I could have been there. I promised them I would go next Sunday. I was looking forward to hearing my uncle preach.

On Sunday, Mike and Rachel and the girls went to church with us. I was kinda nervous about going to church but also excited to see the church my mom grew up in. My grandfather was the pastor then. Aunt had told me the church didn't look the same anymore; they did a lot of remodeling since then. Everyone was so nice to me. When the choir went up to sing, I tried to picture my mother standing up there, and it brought tears to my eyes. I missed her so much.

When Uncle Rob preached, even though I didn't understand a lot of what he was saying, everyone else seem to really enjoy it. They were clapping and raising their hands. It was wonderful.

After church, I went to Scott's mom for dinner.

"Wow, you look great, Tina."

"Well, thank you."

"How was church?" Scott asked.

"Very interesting, I really liked it."

We had a nice visit with his family, and afterward, I drove home, feeling very peaceful about my life. As I was getting ready for bed, Scott called me. "I miss you, Tina, I had a great time last weekend and today. I don't think I can wait until next weekend to see you, so will you have dinner with me tomorrow evening?"

"Sounds prefect. I also had a great weekend. Thanks for inviting me."

"Thanks for going. I will pick you up at six. Until then, have a good night."

After we hung up, I lay there, and my thoughts were only of Scott. I wanted a husband. I wanted kids, and a home of my own with my family. This was what I have wanted since I was a young girl, but what if I was falling for Scott just for those reasons, even though I knew I had feelings for him, and I missed him so much when he was away from me. I didn't even think about Paul anymore.

The next evening, after dinner, we walked to the park and stayed there talking for a long time. I became honest with Scott, and I told him what I wanted—everything. I gave him a chance to walk away because I didn't know at this point what Scott wanted.

"Tina, everything you just told me is exactly what I want. I thought after Lori died, I would never find love—true love anyway. So let me be honest with you, when Lori and I married, right away I told her I wanted to start a family. I guess because I came from a big loving family, and she knew before we married, my dreams, they were also hers. We were married for eighteen months when she became pregnant with Scottie. We were both thrilled. After his birth, I was on cloud nine, so we bought our first house, and everything was great. One day, when Scottie was seven months old, after we put him down for the night, I was watching TV while she took a bath. I will never forget that night as long as I live. She was in the bathroom for a very time, so I went to the door and knocked and asked her if everything was okay. She said she would be right out, so I went back to my movie. But when she walked out, I knew everything was not okay.

"I asked her again, 'Are you okay?'

"She said, 'Yes, I just felt a lump in my breast, but I'm sure it's nothing.'

"She never breastfed Scott, so I just figured it was maybe dried-up milk or something.

"But I told her, 'If you are worried, call and make an appointment tomorrow.'

"'Yeah, I will,' she said.

"I wasn't worried, so I went back to watching TV. But I wish now, I would have taken her into my arm and gave her comfort, but I really didn't think it was anything."

I could see tears in Scott's eyes. I knew he still hurt for Lori. "Scott, you had no way of knowing."

"Tina, can I ask you a question?"

"Yes."

"Am I wasting my time with you? Now that you know where I stand. I've told you everything about me, and I don't want to be hurt either. I have the feeling you are still in love with your ex-husband. Please tell me I'm wrong because I love you, Tina."

"Wow, right to the point. No, I'm not in love with Paul. I know that now. I think I love you too because you are on my mind every moment you are with me. So will you be my boyfriend?" I jokingly said and knocked him off the bench, laughing.

"Oh, it's on now."

I ran as fast as I could, but it was no match for him, he caught me in his arms, right where I wanted to be.

Chapter 41

There wasn't a day that went by that Scott and I wasn't together; either at his mom's house, getting to know his mom and sisters—but best of all, getting to know Scottie and Scott—or at Mike and Rachel's house.

But one evening, after we left Rachel's house, Scott walked me home, and on the front steps of my aunt's house, Scott asked to be his wife. "Tina, will you please marry me. I promise to be the best husband and to make you happy."

"Oh, Scott, you have already made me so very happy, and yes, I will marry you, and I promise I will try with all my heart to make you and Scottie happy."

"Hey, was that our wedding vows?" He laughed.

Lying in my bed that night, my mind was everywhere. I wished so much Mom was here to talk to, to help me plan my wedding. I know she would have loved Scott and Scottie.

Well, after what seemed like hours, I could not sleep, so I went downstairs. Aunt Judy was getting a glass of milk. "You can't sleep either?" she asked.

"No, Scott asked me to marry him."

"Oh my goodness, that's wonderful!" Her face lit up. "Rachel, is going to be so thrilled."

"I know, but I want to wait until we set a date before I tell anyone. Good night, Aunt Judy."

"Good night, dear, try to get some sleep. We have a wedding to plan," she said excitedly.

I watched as she went back upstairs. Wow, I wonder what kind of wedding Scott would want.

The next day was kinda weird for me. Bill called me around noon. "Hey, Tina, do you have a minute?"

"Hi, Bill, yes, what's up?"

"Tina, there is something I wanted to share with you."

"Okay." I was getting a little concerned about where this conversation was going.

"Tina, I met someone, and we are getting married, but I want you to know that your mother will always have that special part of my heart."

"Bill, I'm so happy for you. She is a very lucky lady to be getting you as a husband."

After we hung up, I felt really good that he had called me; it made me happy. Scott and I agreed to buy our house close to his mom since Scottie's school was there, and he didn't want to change that.

Saturday, we went house shopping, and that same day, we found one with the help of a realtor. It was beautiful and prefect, so Scott made the offer that day. I was so excited. It had four bedrooms, two baths, a big kitchen, and a fence in backyard.

On the way back to my aunt's, Scott asked me if I was sure I liked it.

"What's not to like? It's prefect, a prefect neighborhood, and Scottie will stay in his school. I love it, Scott."

"So would you say a nice place to raise our family?"

"Oh, Scott, I would say it's a great place to raise our family."

"I was so happy, my aunt talked me into moving here, so very happy. Okay, let's talk about a date, shall we? The sooner, the better because I can't wait to make you my wife."

"Well, I guess that depends on what kind of wedding you want," I said.

"I want to leave that up to you."

"Well, I have to invite all my family, and with all of them, it will be kinda big, don't you think?"

"Okay, you just tell me what you want me to do, and I will do it. Here is my credit card."

"Wow, you trust me with your credit card?"

"I trust you with my life."

Looking at his phone, we picked our date. I knew I had to tell Rachel soon, but I didn't want to until I could tell her a date. Now I had one. Soon I would be a wife and mother. I knew Rachel would be happy for me, but I had never seen her so excited.

"Oh, Tina, I'm so happy. We have so much to do. You will let me help you, won't you?"

"Yes, I need your help, and I want you to be my matron of honor."

"Yes, yes, I would love to. Thank you for asking me."

"Who else would I ask? You are like the sister I have never had."

Chapter 42

I called Bill the next day to ask him if he would send me mother's wedding dress. He was so excited for me and happy I would be wearing her wedding dress. I was sure this time, it would fit me. Bill said he was also sending me some boxes he packed up for me of my mom's.

About a week later, when I came home from work, the boxes were sitting in the living room. After seeing them, I just lost it. Aunt Judy put her arms around me. "Sweetie, you don't have to do this right now."

I had told Aunt Judy that Bill was sending me mom's things. "It's okay, Aunt, I need to."

She helped me carry the boxes upstairs to my room. "If you need me, I will bè right here."

"Okay, thank you, Aunt Judy."

In the first box was pictures, books, papers, a lot of pictures of Mother and I when I was a baby and as a young child. There were some pictures of my dad, pictures of Mother and Bill's wedding. She was so beautiful. My baby book along with school papers I hadn't known she had kept.

There was an afghan she had made when I was a baby, and a Bible I had never seen before. I opened it up. She had written birthdays in it, date of her marriage to my dad, my name and birthday, all of her sister's and brother's birthdays, her father and mother's birthday, and marriage date, then she wrote: the man that inspires me, Pastor Greg Barton (my dad).

I carefully put everything back in the box and opened the other one where her wedding dress was. It was just as beautiful as I remembered it. Before I tried it on, I called for Aunt Judy to help me.

"Oh, Tina, it's beautiful. You look just like your mom." She started to cry.

The dress fit me prefect.

"Oh, Tina, Rachel and I have been talking. Please let me step into your mother's shoes and give you a wedding."

Now I was crying.

"Okay, I give you full control." We laughed.

After talking with Scott, we all agreed to meet at Mike and Rachel's to talk about the wedding. So after having pizza and a bottle of champagne to celebrate our engagement, we started making plans. We wanted the twins to be our flower girls, Scottie the ringbearer, and his sisters would be my bridesmaid. Scott had already asked Mike to be his best man.

"Uncle Rob, will you please do the ceremony?"

"I would love to, and if you want to be married in the church, your aunt and I would love that."

"Scott and I had already told his mother we wanted to get married in her backyard. It was big with flowers everywhere and a lake, a beautiful place for a wedding."

"That sounds beautiful, and that is fine with us."

My uncle sounded very sincere, so I was okay with not hurting his feelings. So we had everything worked out, and a very happy bride. Every day when I would get home from work, my aunt was talking about the wedding. Everything concerning the ceremony was done—thanks to Rachel, Aunt Judy, and Scott's mom.

Aunt Judy, Scott's sisters, Rachel, and I went to pick out dresses. We had so much fun, trying on dresses and taking crazy pictures. Every girl looked beautiful in their dress.

Chapter 43

Uncle Rob and I were so busy at work. I didn't have time to think about the wedding. Uncle Rob said it was always busy this time of year, but it would slow back down. I hoped so. I hadn't had any time with Scott because we were working every Saturday.

Monday morning was crazy; the main bosses were coming in, and everyone, especially Uncle Rob, was on edge, and I had paperwork up to ears. The only time I saw my uncle was when he popped his head in to see if I had a certain paper ready for him.

Scott called me to invite me to lunch, and as much as I would have loved to escape this madhouse, I told him I couldn't.

Then around noon, Rachel showed up at the office. "Hey, I've come to rescue you for an hour."

"Oh, I'm sorry, I can't. I have too much to do but thank you anyway. It was a very good gesture."

Just then, Uncle Rob came in and gave his daughter a hug. "Why are you here to help us out I assume?"

"Oh, Daddy, you and I both know I would just be in your guys' way. No, I came to take Tina to lunch, but she tells me you are a slave driver."

"Ha ha, go ahead, Tina, you need to eat, and you girls can bring me back something."

"No, Uncle, I can't leave you right now. I will be fine."

"Tina, we will be okay for an hour. Go have a break."

On our way out the door, one of the guys that works there stopped us. "Hey, boss, I just took a phone call in your office. Plans have changed. They will be here in an hour.

I watched the color drain from my uncle's face.

"I will have my part done," I said and headed back to my desk. "Sorry, Rachel."

"No problem. Make it up to me tonight. You and Scott come for supper."

"Okay, I will call him the first chance I get."

For the next half hour, I didn't look up from my computer. I didn't even see Uncle Rob come into the room, but when I did look up, the look on his face was something I would never forget.

"Uncle Rob, what's wrong?"

"Tina, I need you to go home and bring your aunt to the hospital. ASAP."

"What? What are you talking about?"

"Rachel has been in an accident."

"What? When?"

"All I know is she is at the hospital. I don't have any details. I'm leaving now. Tell your aunt she is okay. Don't let her worry."

"Okay, Uncle Rob, I will go now."

Right after I left the building, not far down the road, I could see the road blocked, and police cars everywhere. Oh my god, what is happening? I knew I was going to be sick. I also knew I had to pull myself together before I got home, and I would take another route to the hospital. I couldn't let Aunt Judy see this.

Aunt Judy was cleaning the kitchen when I arrived home.

"Well, hey, this is a nice surprise. Are you home for lunch?"

"No, Aunt, Rachel has been in an accident, but she is okay. Uncle Rob just felt better if I drove you to the hospital."

"What kind of accident?"

"A car accident, but she is okay and probably ready to go home by now," I said with a shaky voice.

On the way there, Aunt Judy was very quiet. I knew she was praying. As soon as we pulled up at the hospital, she was out of the car. I almost had to run to catch up with her before she went through the big doors. Mike must have just arrived because he was at the window, talking to the receptionist as we walked up.

"I'm looking for my wife, Rachel Myers. She was in a car accident."

"Yes, sir, someone will be right with you. If you want to have a seat over there—"

"I don't want to take a seat. I want to see my wife."

Aunt Judy began to cry. A nurse came out and took us down the hall. All I could think about was when I was called to the hospital and took down a hall. I couldn't stop the tears. We were escorted to a room where Uncle Rob and a doctor were at. We all three knew something wasn't right when we saw Uncle Rob.

The doctor began telling us Rachel didn't make it; she was killed instantly. She didn't suffer. She had died at the scene. While they were crying uncontrollably, I sat there in shock. I kept saying over and over, this can't be true. The doctor gave Aunt Judy a shot; it seemed to calm her some, but not her tears. Uncle Rob looked at me and told me to call the family. I said okay. First I went and put my arms around Mike. He sat there with his head down. I called Aunt Kathy, and after the crying, and she calmed down, she said she would call everyone else. Then I called Scott to let him know and also to get a hold of Mike's family, then I went back to where my aunt and uncle were at. I told Aunt Judy her sisters and bothers were on their way. She just looked at me; I don't know if she heard me or not.

I waited outside for everyone so they wouldn't have a problem finding the room. The first person I saw was Scott. I needed him to hold me. My chest was so heavy; the tears were so heavy, but in his arms, I released them. Scott was also crying. This was so horrible. She was leaving a husband behind, and two little girls that adored her. And I was losing my sister.

Whatever the doctor gave Aunt Judy was wearing off; she went from calm to panic. "I want to see my daughter now, where is she?" She cried. Uncle just kelp holding her until she would calm back down.

"Honey, Rachel is sleeping now," he would tell her.

The room became full with family. Mike and Scott were standing in the hall; both men crying. Scott was trying to comfort Mike.

Not that long ago, it was Mike comforting Scott. I just wanted to run away from all of this heartache. I was so sick of hurt and pain and sadness. Then I remembered Sandra and Sara. Who was going to tell them? Who was going to pick them up from school? I didn't even know what time it was. I went in the hall where the guys were standing.

"Mike, I can pick the girls up and keep them until you are ready for them? I won't tell them anything."

"Thank you, Tina," and with remembering his children came a fresh wave of tears.

I looked at Scott and kinda waved goodbye to him, then I left the hospital. I cried all the way home. Rachel was gone, and in an hour, I would be seeing her babies that she would never see again. I went upstairs and knelt by my bed. I prayed for my aunt and uncle and for Kevin, who was on his way home. I prayed for Mike and the girls. I asked God to show me how I could be of help and comfort to them.

After I washed my face, I went to the school. They were happy to see me but wondered why their mom hadn't picked them up. Without answering them, I said, "How would you like to go to Grandma's for a swim?"

"Yay!" they both said at once, "but, Aunt Tina, we don't have our suits. Maybe you can call Mom to bring them down to us?"

As hard as I could, the tears started falling down my face.

"Aunt Tina, what's wrong?" Sara asked me.

"Oh, I'm just having a bad day. It's okay." I lied. I knew it was never going to be okay again.

"It's okay. I'm sure Grandma has suits for us."

After telling the girls Grandma was taking care of some business, I fixed them a snack and carried it outside to the pool deck while they changed into some suits they found.

"How come your not eating, Aunt Tina? Are you still sad?"

"Yes, sweetie, can I have hugs?"

They both gave me hugs. I let them stay in the pool, playing. I watched them, and my mind was everywhere. I knew the wedding would be postponed. I didn't even want a wedding without Rachel.

After an hour, I told them it was time to get out. I didn't know what time Mike would come, and I wanted them dressed. After a while, Sandra said she had homework, so I helped both girls with that, then we made a small supper. I still couldn't eat.

Around 9:00 p.m., when no one still hadn't come home. I took the girls upstairs in the spare room. I just told them daddy wanted them to spend the night with me. They didn't argue when I put a Disney movie on.

Before the girl fell asleep, Mike and Scott and Mike's sister came home. The girls were very excited to see their dad and aunt but wanted to know where their mom was at.

"Hey, girls, guess what?"

"What?" they both said in unison.

"How would you like to spend a few days at Aunt Peggie's with Cindy?"

"Wow, but what about school?"

"It's okay. I will talk to your teacher and let her know."

"Will Mommie take us there?"

"No, Aunt Peggie is taking you now."

"But what about our pj's?" Sandra wanted to know.

"Cindy has pj's just your size, and the three of you can have a pajama party. How does that sound?" their aunt Peggy told them. I could still see the redness in her eyes from crying.

After they left, I made coffee. Mike and Scott sat at the table, talking. So after giving them coffee, I excused myself to give them time to talk.

"No, Tina, please stay," Mike said.

So I sat down.

Mike started to talk.

Chapter 44

"Thank you, guys, for being here for me and letting me stay. I just can't go home right now."

Scott went and put his arms around him. "You know you are welcome here as long as you need."

"Thank you. I know I have to tell the girls, but not right now."

"I just don't understand. The police said a drunk driver crossed the middle line and hit her head on. It was noon time. Who is drunk at noon time?"

We all three were crying.

"Did he or she die?"

As Scott held him, I could see his whole body shaking.

"They took my daughters' mother. They took my life. I hope they died."

Mike's phone rang. After he hung up, he asked Scott to drive him to his mom's house. Not long after they left, Aunt Judy and Uncle Rob came home, along with my other aunts. They led her to the couch, and I went and knelt down beside her.

"Thank you, Tina, for being here and getting the girls."

"You are welcome. Can I get you something to eat or some coffee?"

"No, no, thank you."

She looked so bad. Uncle Rob sat next to her and put his arm around her, and then he put his head down and began to pray.

"Lord, we know you giveth, and you taketh away, but Lord, we want to thank you for the time you have allowed us with our beautiful daughter. Please help us, and please help Mike, Sandra, and Sara.

Lord, they are going to need you in these days that follow. Touch our broken hearts…in Jesus's name."

When I opened my eyes, everyone was standing around with tears in their eyes. It looked like a little peace had touched Aunt Judy; she had stopped crying. When Scott returned, we set up cots for everyone, made snacks, and coffee. I knew the family wouldn't leave their sister for a while, and I wanted to do everything I could for them, just like they did for me.

After everyone was resting, Aunt Kathy was sitting with Aunt Judy. It seemed like Scott always knew when I needed a break. He would take my hand and lead me away and let me cry on his shoulder. I loved him so much.

"Scott, Rachel came by the office to take me to lunch, like she sometimes does. But we were so busy and under the circumstances. I couldn't go, and I kept thinking if I would have gone, maybe I could have seen the car and warned her."

"Oh, Tina, you can't think that way. If you would have been with her, you too could have been killed, and the Lord knows, I couldn't take that."

Chapter 45

The next few days was hard. I was so busy. I didn't have time to think much. The very worst time was when Mike called and asked for Uncle Rob, Scott, and I to come over. It was so hard to go to Rachel's house. How was I going to handle this day?

We all sat on the couch while Mike tried to explain to Sara and Sandra where their mother was. Mike told them that mommie went to heaven to be with Jesus. I could tell they didn't understand.

"But when is mommie coming home?"

"Mommie is not coming home because Jesus needs her to stay with him."

"Grandpa, will my mommie be an angel now?"

"Yes, darling, your mommie is an angel now."

"I want my mom."

Sara started crying. It made us all cry. We tried to be strong for the girls, but this was so sad. I took Sara in my arms. "Sara, mommie will always be with you." I knew that the days that followed, Mike was going to have his hands full with two little girls that would be crying for their mother. Oh my god, how much more can a heart take? I went outside. I didn't want the girls to see me lose it. Scott came out and held me.

"Why? Did God take Rachel? Those girls need her here. Mike needs her here. I just don't understand."

Uncle Rob had come outside, and he heard me. "Tina, we don't know God's ways or his why's, but we just have to trust him."

"But it's so hard to see the people I love suffer so much. Rachel was like my sister."

"I know it is hard, but God will deliver us out of our heartache in time."

I went and gave my uncle a hug. I knew he was trying to be strong and brave for everyone else. But inside, I knew he was hurting so. "You are the strongest man I know, Uncle Rob."

"I don't consider myself strong, but I do know I can do all things in Christ Jesus, who strengthens me. He is with me, and for reasons not for me to know right now, he chose to take my beautiful daughter. I still love him, and I will still praise him because he is my God."

A different kind of tears were now falling down my face. I felt God's love.

There were so many people at the funeral. Scott's mom stayed at home with the twins along with Scottie. Mike didn't think they could handle it. Rachel had a closed casket.

A few days after the funeral, I talked to Scott about our wedding. "I just want to postpone it for a while."

"Tina, I still want to get married. I love you, and I want to be with you every day." But he did come around and agree. That evening, we told Aunt Judy and Uncle Rob.

"No, I won't have it. The wedding will go on as planned. It is what Rachel would have wanted." Aunt Judy was very strong about this.

"I agree with your aunt on this," Uncle Rob said.

So I didn't want to argue with them because it seemed to upset Aunt Judy about the thought of postponing it.

Aunt Kathy was staying with her while we were at work. Aunt Kathy told me she was glad we decided not to postpone the wedding because it gave Aunt Judy something to do to keep her mind busy. She also took the twins with her everywhere she and Kathy went. She just needed to be with them. Scott went to Mike's a lot. It was too hard for me, so I wouldn't go. Mike's mom was staying with them, so the girls were never alone, and since Aunt Judy had them a lot, I got to see them. Their little faces wasn't smiling as much.

Chapter 46

One day, I came home to see all my aunts sitting at the table, making flower arrangements. "What's going on?"

"This is for the wedding, aren't they beautiful?"

"Yes, they are gorgeous."

But I notice, the laughter coming from my aunt Judy. That did my heart glad. She got up and gave me a big hug. "Need more ribbon," she said as she went into the back room.

After Aunt Judy left the room to get yellow ribbon, Aunt Lisa looked at me. "She needs this to keep her mind occupied, so don't you feel guilty. You hear me, you are helping her."

"It's her that has helped me," I said.

"Rachel loved you, and you loved her. You have helped this family as much as you could. I've seen you run around here, trying to take care of everyone. We have needed you these last few weeks, and you have been there for us. This is your wedding and your day, let us do this for you."

I turned my face when Aunt Judy came back into the room. I didn't want her to see me cry. I went upstairs and called Scott.

The next day, I took mother's dress to have it cleaned and pressed, then made my appointment to have my hair done the morning of my wedding.

On Thursday, at Scott's mom's, I watched as the men build a dance floor and hang lights everywhere. It was beautiful. I was glad Mike was here helping.

The next day, the tent was set up. Aunt Judy and the twins were there watching. Everything seemed good, until my aunt came up to me and asked me a question, "Tina, who will be your maid of honor now?"

I told her, "Rachel."

She hugged me, and we both cried.

Scott and I were going back to the little B&B we had went before for our honeymoon, but this time, we would only have one room. Scott and Scottie had already moved into the new house.

At last, everything was ready. After the rehearsal, we didn't go out to eat, instead Scott's sisters gave me a bridal shower, and the guys took Scott out somewhere. There were a lot of women, and I received a lot of gifts.

The next day, after I arrived at my soon-to-be mother-in-law, all my girls were there getting dressed, and everyone awed me when I put my mother's dress on. It was so beautiful, and I felt beautiful in it.

The walk down the aisle began with Uncle Steve on my arm. Everyone walked down with flowers on each side. The twins walked down in front of me; they were so cute. I walked down with flowers everywhere, and then in the front between the girls was a small stand with flowers, a big picture of Rachel, taken on the day she had tried on her maid of honor dress, wearing a big smile. She was beautiful. She was my maid of honor.

Scott had tears in his eyes, but there was still one more surprise for me. After Scott took my hand from Uncle Rob, and I was standing facing him, someone handed him a microphone, and he sung to me.

"Will you give me forever?"

I cried; it was beautiful.

After Uncle Rob said you may kiss the bride, everyone cheered, then all my aunts and uncles lined up, and each gave me a yellow rose in memory of my mom.

Chapter 47

Everyone seemed to have a great time at the reception. There were a lot of people I didn't know. Scott also had a large family and a lot of friends.

Later, when everything was winding down, Scott and I left. We went to a hotel for the night because it was too late to travel. The honeymoon was great. The weather was beautiful. I was so proud to be Scott's wife. I thought of Rachel often, and I could almost see her smiles when she looked at Scott and myself.

Back at home, the sorrow remained. I didn't see so much of Aunt Judy as I did when I lived with them. But of course, I saw Uncle Rob every day at work. On the weekend, we would take the twins and Scottie to the park or a movie. It was on one of those outings that Scott told me he was ready to start our family; I was overjoyed.

Every month, when I found out I wasn't pregnant, I would be so disappointed. But we just kept trying, Scott was always an encouragement to me. Mike was doing good; him and the girls spent a lot of time at Grandma Judy and Grandpa Rob's. It was good for my aunt and uncle ~~good~~ to be with them.

I still kept in touch with Bill. Every once in a while, I called him just to see how he was doing. He seemed happy. He was so happy when I sent him a picture of me in my mother's wedding dress.

It has been three years since Rachel has passed away. Mike and the girls had been going to church with Uncle Rob and Aunt Judy, and that's where he met Tami. Everyone really liked her. She was sweet, and she loved the girls, and the girls loved her. She was their Sunday school teacher.

One day, Mike announced their wedding plans. We were all very happy for them. She had been going to my uncle's church since she was a teenager, so they already loved her. Mike said it would be a small wedding at the church; nothing big and no reception.

Six months after the wedding, we invited them over to dinner, and she told us she was pregnant. I was happy for them, but sad for us. Why weren't I pregnant yet?

Chapter 48

Lying in bed that night, I was talking to Scott about going to the doctor to find out why I wasn't pregnant.

"Okay, go to the doctor, but I'm sure it's because we are just trying too hard. You need to relax and just let nature take its course."

"I know, but it's been almost two years since we have decided to have a baby. I would just feel better if I was checked out."

I called the next day and made an appointment with a gynecologist. I couldn't imagine not having a baby. I have wanted a baby for as long as I could remember. I loved Scottie, and he was my son all the way, but I still wanted a baby.

After talking with the doctor, I felt better. She kinda agreed with Scott, but because we have been trying for so long, she said she wanted to do a typical initial workup that includes a physical exam, blood work that will assess my hormone levels, but in the meantime, relax.

I told Scott about my visit with my gynecologist and about the tests she was going to do. She told me to relax.

"Well, that's good news. Should help you relax some since the doctor and I told you the same thing."

In the meantime, Mike and Tami announced they were having a boy. Mike seemed so excited. I was happy for them, and the twins couldn't wait to have a baby brother. The girls had come so far; they both had their mother's picture on their night stand, and they talked about her often.

I was so happy Tami came into their lives; she was so good with them. Tami and I became friends, but we weren't sisters like

Rachel and I. Mike bought a new house, so I didn't have a hard time going there.

I had the test done, and now just waiting for the results, which seemed to take forever. Scott went with me to the doctor's office. I was a little nervous. After introducing Scott to Dr. Kaye, she began to tell us the test results.

"It seemed you have anovulation."

"What does that mean?" I asked.

"It means lack of ovulation or absent ovulation."

"Sorry, still not sure what that mean." I didn't want to sound stupid, but I just wanted answers I could understand.

"Ovulation, which is the release of an egg from the ovary must happen in order to achieve pregnancy, and if ovulation is irregular but not completely absent, this is called oligoovulation, both onovulation and oligoovulation are kinds of ovulatory dysfunction."

"Well, bottom line, what can be done for me to have a baby?"

"You can try fertility drugs, but there is no guarantees."

"So, Dr. Kaye, are you saying I can never get pregnant?"

"No, I'm not saying that. I'm saying your chances are very low… that you will become pregnant on your own. I wish I had better news for you."

We thanked her and left. On the way home, I couldn't help but cry.

The next few months, I cried every time I got my period. But as time went by, I got used to the idea: I wasn't going to have a baby. Scott was great through it all. He pretended it didn't bother him, but I knew the truth. But I did have my little family that I was thankful for. I had a great husband, a son, and a beautiful home, also a very large family that I didn't have before, so life was good.

I loved babysitting the girls and little Michael. We took family vacations together. We were always at some family member's house. I loved Scott's mom; she treated me like her daughter. I had always wanted siblings when growing up because I had always felt all alone when my mom was at work. Now I had so many. I made sure Scottie was always around his cousins.

Chapter 49

Scott and I decided to go away for our eighth anniversary. He told me he would take me anywhere I wanted to go. It didn't take much thought for me. "I want to go home. I want to visit my mom's grave, and I want to visit Bill."

"Okay, your old hometown it is."

I knew he was trying to say that wasn't my home anymore, but here was my home. Scottie stayed with his grandma.

Just driving back into that city brought tears to my eyes. It seemed like a lifetime ago. After we got settled in our hotel room, we went to Bill's house. His wife was a very good person; she kept insisting on making us dinner. Bill looked so much older but seemed happy, and he acted so happy to see me.

After that, we went to the cemetery. Bill had told me that he takes care of it, and it looked like he was doing a good job. This was the first time I had been here. Scott put his arm around me, but I didn't cry. In a few minutes, he went to the car, so I could talk to her. I knelt down, and I told her everything about my life. I told her how much I missed her, then I told her goodbye.

Scott was standing beside the car, waiting for me. After we got back to the hotel, Scott said he was going to take a nap.

"Okay, I'm going to drive around for a little while."

"No, I will go with you."

"No, Scott, please. I just need this time alone."

"I don't like the idea of you going alone."

"Scott, take a nap. Remember I grew up here. I will be fine."

"Okay but keep your cell on and don't be gone long."

As I drove through town, so much has changed in such a short time. I drove to the plant where I used to work. I missed my mother. How many times had I pulled up here and seen her car parked here. The pain of loss was so strong. I knew I had make a mistake coming here.

My old house looked so small. Then I remembered it; there were two cars in the driveway.

I wondered who lived there, and I hoped if there were children living there, there were more than just one.

I felt such a sadness looking at the house I grew up in and remembering all the unhappiness there from when I was a child to when I was a married woman—all the hurt Paul had caused me.

Scott was right: this is not my home.

Chapter 50

On my way back to the hotel, even though I had told myself a thousand times I would not, I drove by the house that Paul and Joan had purchased when he left. I don't know what I was trying to accomplish.

I drove by very slowly. I saw a boy on a bike, and I knew right away, it was Paul's son. He looked just like Paul, so they had a son. I was so busy looking at the boy I hadn't noticed I had come to a complete stop in front of the house.

When I turned to go, I looked right into the eyes of Joan. She was smiling at me and waving her arms, wanting me to get out. She seemed so happy like a little girl. Against my better judgment, I pulled into the drive.

"I remember you…you are my mom's friend that owns the store with the candy animals."

What is wrong with her? She had on cut-off shorts, very unevenly cut. Her hair looked like it hadn't been brushed in a very long time, and she smelled badly.

A lady came out and took her by the hand. "Come on, Joan, you know you are not to be by the driveway."

After leading her away, I looked for the boy, but he was gone.

The lady came over to me. "Can I help you?"

All this time, I hadn't said a word, just stood by my car. "My name is Tina. Joan and I were friends a long time ago. Can you tell me what happened to her?"

"Well, I can't, I'm just her caregiver."

"Can you tell me where her husband is?"

"As far as I know, Joan has never been married, but I'm not allowed to discuss Joan. Like I said, I'm just her caregiver. You can wait until her mom gets home which should be any minute if you want."

Joan didn't come over to where I was, and I didn't see her son anymore. He must have gone into the house. I was only there for a few minutes when Joan's mother came home. She looked at me in shock. "Tina, is that you?"

"Hi, how are you?" I asked.

"Really surprised to see you here. Did you move back?"

"Oh no, just visiting. I came by to see Joan," I lied. Her mom looked so old.

"Well, I can't imaging you would ever want to see Joan again after what she did to you," she stated.

"That was a long time ago. Can you tell me what happened to her?"

"We are not really sure. When she was pregnant with Jayson, she was out shopping and suffered some kind of illness. She couldn't breathe and was unconscious for a long time. She lost a lot of oxygen to her brain. They did an emergency C-section, so now she has to have a caregiver at all times.

"What about Paul?"

"When Joan got sick, that sorry loser left. He only saw Jayson when he was born. We haven't heard from him until recently. Jayson has been talking to him, and in fact, is going to go live with him next month. As much as I don't want to, Joan is going into an adult foster care home, and I'm moving to Indiana with my sister. My health is getting to bad to work and take care of Joan anymore.

"I hope one day, you can forgive Joan for what she did to you. You were her friend, and it was very wrong."

"I already have. I wish the best for Joan and Jayson and for you." I gave her a hug goodbye. I told Joan goodbye, but I wasn't sure she heard me. She just looked at me and continued to eat her ice cream. I drove away, and I knew today I had found closure because I truly forgave Joan.

Chapter 51

When I got back to our hotel room, I heard water running and knew Scott was taking a shower, so I got undressed and got into the shower with my husband.

"Sorry I'm late, but I ran into an old friend."

He took me in his arms. "That's okay, as long as it wasn't an old boyfriend," he joked, then he put his hands on my bulging stomach. "Hey, did you feel that? She likes showers."

"No, she is going to be a bubble bath girl, just like her mommie and grandma Dana.

Just when Tina finds happiness, death once again takes its toll on her family. Find out how she must overcome the battles of sickness, death, marriage and motherhood in *Empty Vows*.

About the Author

Brenda is retired. She has four children, ten grandchildren, and three great-grandchildren. She is married to Duane Rogers together with their two Maltese-mixed dogs. They reside in Michigan. Besides spending time with family, she loves to read, being active in her church and having a special love and relationship with God.

CPSIA information can be obtained
at www.ICGtesting.com
Printed in the USA
FSHW021954130719
59885FS